I shouldn't be doing this.

But Sophie must have felt the change in him and she lifted her head to look at him to check that he was okay.

Theo looked down into her eyes. Such a deep blue. Like a clear Caribbean sea. She held such wonder in those eyes of hers. Such concern. Such hope, such…desire? He looked down at her mouth, her lips parting as she breathed.

Would it be wrong? To take advantage of this moment? Should he be a gentleman and walk away?

"Sophie, we shouldn't do this."

He saw her glance at his mouth and he wanted to kiss her so much it almost tore him in two. But she wasn't his. Wasn't meant to be his, and this wasn't how friends should be with each other. So why was his body telling him to throw caution to the wind and friendship be damned? That kissing her would be the most wonderful thing in this world?

Dear Reader,

For five years, I volunteered as a community first responder on my small island of Hayling, responding to 999 calls and providing life-saving medical care until paramedics arrived and took over. During my time volunteering, I worked with a lot of rapid-response paramedics, who were all marvelous and really inspired me to write a story involving a rapid-response paramedic one day. I just had to wait for the right story.

So along came Sophie Westbrook, heavily pregnant and determined to not let anything stand in her way. I adore Sophie. She's strong. A badass! And I knew I needed a hero who could break down the walls around her heart. Theo Finch, ex-army, wise guy and student paramedic, was the perfect choice!

I do hope you love their journey to a happy-ever-after!

Love,

Louisa xxx

A BABY TO RESCUE
THEIR HEARTS

———

LOUISA HEATON

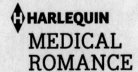

HARLEQUIN
MEDICAL
ROMANCE

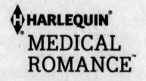

HARLEQUIN®
MEDICAL ROMANCE™

Recycling programs
for this product may
not exist in your area.

ISBN-13: 978-1-335-40453-4

A Baby to Rescue Their Hearts

Copyright © 2021 by Louisa Heaton

This edition published by arrangement with Harlequin Books S.A.

For questions and comments about the quality of this book,
please contact us at CustomerService@Harlequin.com.

Harlequin Enterprises ULC
22 Adelaide St. West, 40th Floor
Toronto, Ontario M5H 4E3, Canada
www.Harlequin.com

Printed in U.S.A.

Louisa Heaton lives on Hayling Island, Hampshire, with her husband, four children and a small zoo. She has worked in various roles in the health industry—most recently four years as a community first responder, answering 999 calls. When not writing, Louisa enjoys other creative pursuits, including reading, quilting and patchwork—usually instead of the things she *ought* to be doing!

Books by Louisa Heaton

Harlequin Medical Romance

Reunited by Their Pregnancy Surprise
Their Double Baby Gift
Pregnant with His Royal Twins
A Child to Heal Them
Saving the Single Dad Doc
Their Unexpected Babies
The Prince's Cinderella Doc
Pregnant by the Single Dad Doc
Healed by His Secret Baby
The Icelandic Doc's Baby Surprise
Risking Her Heart on the Trauma Doc

Visit the Author Profile page at Harlequin.com.

To the real baby Cassidy—stay strong.
And to my dad. I will always love you. xxx

CHAPTER ONE

SOPHIE FIGURED THERE were three different types of men in the world.

The first kind she knew very well. Those men told you that they loved you, that you were the centre of their world, their beating heart— but then they left you because you'd become 'complicated' or 'needed more' or they thought they'd found someone *'easier'*.

The second kind were the nice guys. Those were rare—in short supply. In fact, she wasn't sure they truly existed, having never met one herself, but she'd heard her friends talk about them. The boys next door, who never seemed to be anything special at first, but were always snapped up by other, luckier women, before you realised who'd been living under your nose all that time.

And then there was the third kind. The kind who were often seen posing as half-naked fire-fighters for calendars, holding a cute puppy whilst their biceps, pecs and six-packs gleamed with oil. All square jaws and designer stubble, with perfect white teeth and a sexually charged smoulder.

And one of those was currently walking into her ambulance station.

'Wowser…' she breathed, trying to hide her stare, pretending to check the equipment in the back of her rapid response vehicle, occasionally peeking over the roof as if to confirm that he was actually real and not a hallucination.

His green paramedic uniform fitted him very well. A little too well, in fact. Surely it was against the law to look that good? Or maybe it just fitted him perfectly but her pregnancy-induced hormones, which had been starved of male attention for months and months, were transforming what she could actually see. Sex-starved goggles, rather than beer goggles…

He was the big three—tall, dark and handsome—with a killer smile that did strange things to her insides as, from behind her car, she watched him conversing with her boss over by his office.

She couldn't hear their conversation and she was curious. She *was* expecting a student paramedic to join her for a couple of weeks—but there was no way this guy was the student she was expecting! In her experience students were younger, fresh out of the lecture hall, their faces filled with eagerness and apprehension. Nervous. Anxious.

This guy was sure of himself, confident and more mature, and possibly in his thirties. The prime of his life. No doubt he was virile and physical and...

Taken. He's taken—obviously! I mean, come on, look at the guy!

She blew out a calming breath. Probably he was someone from higher up the chain who'd suddenly decided to do an inspection, or something. Nothing to do with her. Nothing that—

Her boss, Pete, laughed at something the guy said and nodded in Sophie's direction.

She dipped down beneath the roof of the car, cursing silently. Had they noticed her staring?

That would be embarrassing.

She yanked open the drawer that held the adult masks and counted them once again, her mind racing at what was going on as her cheeks bloomed with heat and desire. She'd expected a lot of things from pregnancy, like a huge belly and puffy ankles and weird food cravings, but these sexual feelings all the time... It was typical that she turned out to be one of *those*, when there was no bloke around to sort them out for her!

Was the new guy from head office or something?

Was he here to tell her she'd have to go on maternity leave early?

Because she refused to! She would work for as long as she could. Now that she was on her own she couldn't afford to take time off for longer than she needed to—and besides, she still felt fit. She could lift, she could run, she could do CPR…all the things required of a rapid response paramedic. It would be madness to take someone with her skills off the road and tell her to go and knit bootees or something.

'Hi.'

She jumped, and banged her head on the roof of the car, wincing and feeling her cheeks colour. Rubbing at her head, she peered over the top. 'Hey.'

Firefighter Calendar Guy stood by the driver's door, smiling at her. 'You okay?'

'I'm fine, thank you." She rubbed hard at her bruised scalp. "Can I help you?'

'I'm Theo Finch.'

Theo. Of course. A guy like him *would* have a beautiful name. Something that rolled off the tongue…that would sound perfect as she breathed it out, her lips caressing the name as they brushed against his neck…

Sophie cleared her throat. 'Pleased to meet you, Theo. What can I do for you?'

She could think of many things he could do for *her*, and her brain thoughtfully provided the imagery for all of those and more as she tried to appear nonchalant and carefree and as innocent as a nun.

'I'm your student. I'm shadowing you for the next month?'

She almost laughed. A nervous, hysterical laugh that would have sounded as if she deserved to be assessed by a mental health clinician. But she managed to hold it in.

This guy was her *student*? How the hell was she supposed to concentrate and do her job with *him* around?

'My student? I'm sorry,' she said with a laugh, 'I was expecting someone more...'

'Green-looking?'

She smiled. They all looked green. It was the uniform. But she didn't want to look at his uniform. Moulded as it was to his masculine, muscled form. Because all that made her think about was what lay beneath it...

She tried to work out how she would cope with this new development in her life. Realised she would just have to deal with it. Besides, he wouldn't be interested in her in *that way*. She looked like a beached whale, and men like him dated sylph-like girls with big hair, big boobs, talon-sharp fake nails and no real eyelashes of their own.

And, for the record, she wasn't really interested in him, either!

I've sworn off men. My life is just going to be me and my daughter. That's it. Nothing else needed. Except maybe one hot night occasionally, because why not?

She was a grown woman. She had needs.

She looked at him more intently, her gaze taking in his dark-lashed blue-green eyes, the beautiful curve of his lips, the fine dark hair covering his muscled forearms.

I need to get a grip. That's what I need.

'Hi, I'm Sophie Westbrook.'

Theo had been waiting for this day for a long time. He'd always been one of those guys who'd never quite thought about what he wanted from life, growing up. There'd never seemed time to be worrying about career choices—not when he'd had to be the man in his family and help look after his ailing mother and three younger sisters.

A career had seemed like something *other* people talked about, and when he'd had to meet with the careers advisor at his secondary school he'd told the softly spoken woman behind the large glasses that he'd probably just look for some menial work to fit in around helping run the house.

The advisor had told him that he was something called 'a carer', and that he was entitled to support, but somehow none of that had actually panned out. His mother had not been a woman to accept charity, so Theo had simply carried on carrying on—until his mother had died and his sisters had flown the nest and he'd gone to an army recruiting office and signed up.

But his time in the army, following in his father's footsteps, had not been what he'd hoped it would be. He'd thought he would find routine and rules—something that would take care of him for a change. Instead he'd found himself caring intensely for his new family—the other soldiers in his battalion. Losing some of them in Afghanistan had been brutal—totally unexpected—and he'd left before he could lose any more.

You're a carer.

Those were the words he kept hearing, over and over in his skull, and he knew them to be right. It was all he'd done. But how to do that in life, without getting attached to people?

He'd considered becoming a doctor, but the training lasted years and years and he wasn't sure he had that in him. Being a nurse was something he was familiar with, but the idea of being on a ward and getting to know his patients over time, caring for them, worrying about them, seemed too much.

He'd had enough of sitting by someone's bedside watching them die, trying to convince them to take their medicine and holding their hands through nights of pain and discomfort. It hurt too much. He'd known he needed something different. Something less attachment-forming. So he'd decided on being a paramedic.

He'd get the drama, the adrenaline rush that he was used to from being in the army, and he would get to care for people, to try and make them better, and then he could walk away. No long-term commitment needed. No getting to know someone before watching them die. No having to deal with that loss. If a patient died on him? Yes, it would be sad, but not as upsetting as losing someone he'd come to care for deeply.

The first few weeks of university had been fascinating, and now he was here on his very first placement—and it was with a rapid response paramedic. Just the kind of thing he imagined doing himself. Working solo in a vehicle like this, or maybe being a paramedic on a motorbike?

And he'd been placed with *Sophie*.

She was cute. In fact, she was more than

that. His first thought had been that she was strikingly beautiful. Dark blonde hair that fell in waves to her shoulders, large blue eyes, a slightly wonky smile that was wide and caused her eyes to gleam, and…

Sophie came out from behind the vehicle and the first thing he saw—couldn't help but see—was her enormous abdomen, swollen with a baby.

'You're *pregnant*.' Then he coloured at stating the obvious!

She smiled. 'And you've just made your first assessment and diagnosis. We'll make a paramedic of you yet.'

He laughed. 'I'm sorry, I—'

'Is my being pregnant a problem for you?' She was looking at him curiously, her head tilted to one side in a challenge.

'No!'

'Good."

'I'm sorry, I didn't mean to blurt that out. I just wasn't expecting—'

'To be lumbered with an elephant?' She smiled.

Theo let out a breath and then laughed, holding out his hand once again. 'Can we start over? Hi, I'm Theo.'

She reached out to take his hand and laughed. 'Sophie. Pleased to meet you, Theo. Now, shall

I show you how we check the vehicle to make sure it's roadworthy before we go out on shift?'

He was very relieved that she'd allowed him her grace. He couldn't believe he'd been so clumsy to start with. He was lucky that she was as kind as she was. 'Yes, please.'

He let go of her hand reluctantly, noticing she wore no ring on either hand, before following her to the rear of the vehicle.

'First we do a stock check and make sure the oxygen and Entonox tanks are full and any medications are well within their use-by date. There's a checklist here that we work through.' She pulled out a clipboard and gave it to him. 'I've already gone through it, but we'll go through it again as it will be good for you to check with me and familiarise yourself with the whereabouts of each item, in case I need you to find something for me when we're out on a shout. Okay?'

He nodded and pulled his pen from his sleeve pocket, feeling happier now that they were getting down to business, after the awkwardness of before.

Sophie had barely pulled out of the station and signed on for duty with the control room when a call came through. A young girl had been thrown from her horse.

'Six zero two, responding,' said Sophie.

'Thank you, six zero two. HEMS seven four eight also en route,' said the calm voice over the system.

'You see that button there?' Sophie pointed at a switch on the dashboard.

'Yes.'

'Press it.'

Theo reached forward and depressed the switch and the sirens began to sound. 'Blues and twos.' He smiled.

Sophie checked both ways at a junction before cutting through the traffic, making sure that everyone knew they were there and had stopped, or were stopping, before she pulled out and began to drive down the road towards the motorway that would get them to Cobham the fastest.

At this speed she had to concentrate, because— unfortunate as it was—not everyone on the roads responded in the correct manner when an emergency vehicle was coming up behind them, lights blazing and sirens blaring. She'd lost count of the number of drivers who never bothered to look in their mirrors and didn't get out of the way. And if she'd got a pound for every driver who had cut her up or refused to let her pass she'd be a millionaire by now, sitting on a baby-soft couch at home being hand-fed grapes by a half-naked Adonis, whilst another bronzed god wafted her with an ostrich feather fan.

'Hopefully you've never travelled at these speeds before?' she asked Theo.

'On a road? No.'

She guessed he meant that he'd been in a plane, or a high-speed train, or something. 'By the time you've finished your placement with me you'll be more than familiar with some of the mistakes other drivers make. If I had my way, I'd make it part of the practical driving test to have to deal with emergency vehicles whilst out on the road.'

'They're that bad?'

'Like you wouldn't believe! Lots of people are very good at pulling over and getting out of our way, but sometimes they pull over in the wrong place—like on blind corners, forcing us to go head-on into the other lane, not knowing what's coming. It slows down our response time, and response times are everything.'

'We have to get there within seven minutes?'

'For a category one call, yes.'

'What are those, usually?'

'Anything considered life-threatening or something that might need immediate intervention.'

'And is getting there in seven minutes always doable?'

'It depends on many things—traffic, time of day, roadworks…'

'Lots of variables come into play?'

'They most certainly do.'

'Do you think we'll get to this call on time?'

She glanced at the clock on her dashboard. 'Most definitely.'

It was a matter of pride for Sophie and all the other paramedics she knew who worked damned hard to meet response times, ensuring not only patient care, but also the safety of themselves and other road users.

'Have you had much experience of patient care?' she asked.

It would be good to know if he had. He was older than the students she usually mentored, so it was likely he had seen more in life. Experienced more. Hopefully he wasn't the type to faint at the sight of blood.

'Some.'

Had she noticed a hint of terseness in his voice? 'Good. When we get there, you must wear a jacket that says you're an observer. You can help me carry equipment and things, but no rushing forward until I've assessed the situation and know that it's safe for us to approach. At *any* call—okay?'

'I know. They gave us health and safety lectures at university.'

'Lectures are one thing. Real life is another. Especially when all your instincts are screaming at you to forget safety and just get in there and help.'

She saw him nod in her peripheral vision.

'What sort of danger would you expect at this call?' he asked.

'Well, she's fallen off a horse, so the horse might still be around. We'll need to make sure it's contained—especially if HEMS are going to be landing.' He'd know that HEMS was the Helicopter Emergency Medical Service. 'Any good with animals?'

He gave a small laugh. 'Not really had the opportunity.'

She smiled. Theo was easy to talk to when she didn't have to look directly at him. She could pretend he was just another guy. Just her work partner. Her student. He was here to learn, and as long as she stuck to educating him and nothing else, she should be absolutely fine. *Keep things serious...no flirting.* That was doable, right? Looking directly at him was another thing. Looking into those come-to-bed eyes of his would be distracting.

The turn-off for Cobham came into view and she indicated, checking her mirrors and watching the traffic on the slip road before cleaving her way through the centre at the lights to take the turning they needed. Thankfully, the drivers there got out of her way, and she quickly zipped past a big supermarket on her left and drove through Cobham cautiously, before taking the road she needed for the farm they'd been called to on the outskirts. Her GPS system showed her that she was about a minute away, and above her she could see a helicopter coming in from the east.

Tipton Farm was atop a small hill and had a long, rutted driveway which she drove down cautiously, trying to avoid the potholes and puddles. To one side was a field of cows and on the other a crop of some kind that she couldn't identify. It stood quite tall—almost waist-height, if she had to guess.

At the end of the driveway, a woman flagged them down. 'Harriet is down there!' She pointed to a small path.

'Thank you.' Sophie drove towards the path and parked. 'This is where we disembark,' she told Theo. 'Hope you've got a strong back—the bags weigh a ton.'

She quickly radioed through to Control to say that she'd arrived on scene, and then she got out of the vehicle and opened up the boot. She passed Theo the jump bag and equipment she thought they might need and grabbed a pair of gloves as well.

'Ready?' She took a moment to smile at him, and was rewarded with a dazzling smile that did things to her insides.

Concentrate.

She quickly looked away as they began walking towards the patient. In front of them was a small huddle of people, gathered around somebody on the ground. A woman held a beautiful chestnut-coloured horse by its reins off to one side.

The people stood back to make space for her and Sophie quickly assessed the situation. Her patient—Harriet—was lying flat on her back, covered in some coats that had been laid over her. She wore a riding helmet, which was good, but she looked pale. The ground seemed solid and there didn't appear to be any hazards that might harm anybody.

'Could we get rid of the horse? The air ambulance will most probably land in this field next to us, so it would be safer for all involved if it was back in its stable.'

The woman holding the horse nodded and began to lead the animal away.

Sophie put on her gloves, crouched next to her patient and smiled. 'Hello, Harriet, my name's Sophie and I'm a paramedic. How old are you, sweetheart?'

'Fourteen.' Harriet's teeth chattered. Most probably from shock.

'Can you tell me what happened?'

As Harriet spoke, telling Sophie how her horse had been walking quite sedately down the path when it had been startled by a deer jumping out from the underbrush and had thrown her off onto her back, Sophie was assessing her patient's body by eye, mentally working out the height of her patient's fall, how the impact might have happened and what she would need to check for.

'And what hurts…if anything?'

'My back and my hips.'

'And if you had to rate your pain from zero to ten, with zero being no pain and ten being the worst you've ever felt in your life, where would you say you were?'

'About a s-s-six?' Her teeth were still chattering.

'Okay, Harriet, you're doing wonderfully. I'm just going to check you out, so you'll feel me touching you, but I'll try not to hurt you. Is that okay? Don't nod—just say yes or no.'

'Yes.'

Sophie began her primary survey of Harriet. The helmet was not cracked or broken, but that didn't mean Harriet hadn't taken a blow to the head when she'd landed. She felt nothing out of place in the girl's neck or shoulders, arms or legs, but there was tenderness, as Harriet had mentioned, around her pelvis. It was possible it was broken, or there was an injury to her back.

She reached into her bag and got out her SATS probe and slipped it onto Harriet's finger. Whilst she waited for it to give her the result she got out the Entonox—a mixture of nitrous oxide and oxygen.

'Just breathe in and out for me…this should help with your pain.'

Behind them, she could hear the *whump-whump* of the helicopter's blades as it got closer, and she could feel the downdraft as it lowered to the ground.

She carried on with her assessment. Harriet's oxygen levels were good. Her pulse rate was a bit high, but that was understandable in this situation. She'd had an accident. She was scared. In pain. She didn't know what was going to happen.

Sophie tried to shield Harriet from the worst of the downdraft and then, as the engine whined, she took hold of Harriet's head and held it still. 'Some nice doctors are about to arrive now. They'll most likely ask you a few questions, and then they'll want to put you in a collar to support your neck and get you on a spinal board for a trip to the hospital.'

'In the helicopter?'

Sophie smiled. 'Absolutely. Ever been in one before?'

'No.'

'Well, you're about to.'

Sophie glanced up to look at Theo and make sure he was okay. He was doing as she'd asked. Standing back and observing, looking at the patient on the ground with a mixture of concern and apprehension.

The HEMS doctor arrived and she gave a brief hand-over of her findings and let him take control. He was the senior on the scene, though as she was the one with cervical control of Harriet's neck she would be the one to control her log-roll onto the spinal board that was arriving.

'Theo? You need to watch how we do this so next time you can help.'

'I can help you now. I did this in the army.'

The army? Okay, so that explained the proud way he walked, the upright posture, the confidence. 'Okay, you can grab her legs. You know where to hold them?'

He quickly positioned himself by Harriet's legs and placed his hands in the right position, giving her confidence in what he'd said.

'Good. Once we've got the pelvic brace on we'll need you, okay?'

'I'll be ready.'

The HEMS doctor quickly tightened a brace around Harriet's pelvis. 'She's secure.'

'Okay, let's roll to the right on the count of three, then. One, two, *three*.'

They rolled Harriet so that the spinal board could be placed underneath her. Then, on another count, they rolled her onto her back. Sophie checked with her small team to make sure everyone was happy before they log-rolled her to the left and back again.

'Right, we're just going to get you all strapped in, Harriet, and then you're going to go in the helicopter with Dr Howard—okay?'

'Thank you.' Harriet smiled and giggled slightly. It was a nervous giggle, but at least it showed the Entonox was doing its stuff.

'Mum and Dad? Harriet will be going to Kingston Hospital. There's no room for you in the helicopter. Are you able to make your own way there?'

Her parents nodded, looking anxious.

Sophie reached out to lay a hand upon the mother's arm. 'She's in good hands.'

'She's all we've got…'

Sophie wished *she'd* had parents who had

worried as much as Harriet's parents seemed to. She was a lucky girl.

With the HEMS team and Theo, she helped carry Harriet across the field to the waiting helicopter. The HEMS doctor swapped Sophie's Entonox for their own and gave her back her canister. Then she and Theo hurried back to their vehicle and began packing their equipment away.

'How did you find that?' she asked him, smiling, hoping that he had loved it as much as she did.

'It was good!'

'You enjoyed it?'

'I did. Which is strange when you think about it. Enjoying someone else being in pain…'

'But we're here to help. Without us they'd be in a lot more pain or distress. You enjoyed watching someone receive help and feel better. Not the fact that she was in pain.'

He nodded. 'Yeah… You think she'll be okay?'

'I hope so. She had feelings in all four limbs… could move her toes. We can only hope she's just suffered bruising from the fall, but there's always the possibility that there are injuries we couldn't see.'

'And that's why we prepare for the worst?'

'But hope for the best. Yes.'

A car passed them. Harriet's parents on their way to the hospital.

Sophie and Theo both waved. Then she turned back to consider him. Her interest in him was rearing its head once again. 'So...the army, huh?'

He nodded. 'Yeah.'

'What made you leave?'

Theo shrugged. 'I'd had enough.'

Okay. Short and sweet.

'Didn't you enjoy it?'

'I did, but...'

He looked away from her then, and she saw a darkness in his eyes that made her wonder if he'd been hurt in some way.

'It was just time to make a change,' he said.

She nodded. Something had affected him. She could tell. Something he didn't want to talk about. It intrigued her to know that this stunning man at her side might look as if he had no troubles in the world, and as if his life was as perfect as his hair, but in reality he was just as screwed up as the rest of them.

'Was it a hard adjustment, being a civilian again?'

'A bit. But a friend of mine got me a job as a rock-climbing instructor, so that's what I was doing up until going to university.'

'You like being active?'

She smiled, imagining him climbing the sheer face of a mountain. Bare-chested, his beautiful trim waist holding a cascade of ropes and clips and...what were those things called...? *Carabiners?* His muscles would be straining and flexing under his skin, droplets of sweat dripping down his—

'I do.'

'You look like it.'

She'd said the words without thinking. Now he would think that she'd been staring at his body—which she had. But he didn't need to know that.

She felt flustered. 'I mean, I can tell you do a lot of physical things.'

Oh, God, it's getting worse! Shut your mouth, Sophie!

Fortunately, he just smiled at her.

'You go to the gym a lot?' she asked, feeling embarrassed.

'Yes. I do. You?'

She rubbed at her abdomen. 'Oh, sure! Can't you tell?' Sophie laughed in disbelief at herself. 'I used to. But I'm more of a swimmer, to be honest.'

He glanced down at her belly. 'So no doubt the little one will be, too?'

She grimaced. 'Not so little. She feels enormous already and I've still got weeks to go.'

'She? You know it's a girl?'

Sophie nodded. 'I wanted to know. So I could plan…get things sorted. I like to know what's going to happen ahead of time—that way I can account for contingencies and things going wrong.'

'Are you a pessimist?'

'No. I like to think I'm a realist. Life so far has taught me that just when I think I've got everything sorted, and my life is on an even keel, something will come along to ruin it. Anyway, enough about me—let's get this stuff sorted.'

She felt as if his questions were leading her down a route to where she'd end up spilling all her personal secrets, and she didn't want him thinking that she was a great mess of a human being who had screwed up entirely.

He was her student and she was his mentor. He didn't need to know anything about her. Not really. Realistically, he'd be in her life for a short time and then he'd go. All she'd be to him was a memory.

She wanted him to look back at that memory with fondness. To smile when he recalled her, the rapid response paramedic he'd done his first placement with, and remember how much fun she'd been. Not to think of it as a time he'd spent with a mentor who'd done nothing but complain about her life and whinge. Besides, that wasn't who she was. She tried to remain upbeat. Because anything else just led to depression and self-pity and she refused to go down that road.

Sophie showed Theo how all the equipment they'd used went into a clinical waste container. Then she restocked the jump bag and got Theo to check the level of Entonox the way she'd showed him back at the station.

'It's half full.'

'Okay. Let's get going.'

They got back into the car and Sophie radioed through to Control that they were free from the scene and available.

'Thank you, six zero two. Everything all right?'

'All good. Patient with HEMS. Suspected back or pelvic fracture.'

'Poor kid. Let's hope she's okay.'

'I hear you.'

'Are you available to attend an RTC on the A3 near the Esher turn-off?'

'We most certainly are. On our way.'

'Thank you, six zero two. Safe travels.'

'Thank you, Control.' Sophie smiled at Theo. 'When we get back towards the centre of Cobham, do you want to light us up?'

'Sure.' He nodded.

Sophie began the slow drive down the farm's

bumpy driveway that tested the suspension of the vehicle, and it wasn't long before the blues and twos were creating a clear passageway for them through the mid-afternoon traffic.

CHAPTER TWO

THEO HAD ENJOYED his first day with Sophie. In fact, he was pretty amazed by her. She was so on the ball, professional…and, boy, was she fit for a woman in the latter stage of her third trimester!

She could carry hefty bags of gear, run up flights of stairs, help lift patients and control onlookers who wanted to get in the way as if it was nothing. It was almost as if there were times in the day when she seemed to forget that she was pregnant. The only sign that she was, was her huge belly, and the habit she had of occasionally having to chew on some red liquorice, which she'd just admitted was a craving at the moment.

'I know all about pregnancy cravings,' he told her.

Sophie looked at him. 'Oh?'

'My younger sisters all had them when they were pregnant.'

'How many sisters?'

'Three. I'm the oldest and the only boy.'

'So you're an uncle? To how many?'

'I have four nieces and two nephews—and let me tell you red liquorice is a nice, normal craving compared to some of the things my sisters wanted to eat.'

'Such as?'

'Leonora craved cheesy puffs in chocolate ice cream with her latest, Hazel wanted fishfingers on waffles, but it was Martha who craved sticks of chalk.'

'Chalk?' Sophie laughed.

'Yeah. The doctors said it was something called pica?'

'I've heard of that. So I should be thankful I'm normal, then?'

He nodded and smiled.

'First time for everything, I guess.'

They were checking the car before handing it over to the next paramedic for the night shift.

'You seem normal to me,' he said.

'You don't know anything about me.'

'I know some things.'

'Like…?'

She stopped to consider him over the roof of the car and he couldn't help but notice that, even though they'd just completed a nine-hour shift in which they'd attended call after call,

Sophie looked just as good as she had first thing that morning.

He paused to think, wanting to keep this professional. 'I know that you're very good at your job. You're a good teacher. You explain things very well. I know you're heavily pregnant but you don't let it affect you at work.'

He noticed her smile and suddenly wondered if he'd gone too far, giving his attractive female colleague compliments… He needed her to know that he wasn't interested in her in that way, even if he did feel attracted to her. Perhaps if he showed that he knew she was unavailable…

'I hope when you get home you can have a good rest. Put your feet up, let someone cook you a nice meal…'

'Fat chance of that. I live alone.' She smiled wryly. 'What about you, Theo? Who do you go home to?'

'No one.'

She seemed to consider this for a moment, and he wondered what was running through her head. And why was *she* alone? For some reason the idea of that made him feel a little sad. Did she not live with the father of her child? Surely that would change when the baby arrived? Or was she going to be a single mother? That didn't seem right to him either.

Sophie was such a nice person. Surely she was in a relationship? He needed her to be in a relationship. Because that way she was totally unavailable and he didn't have to worry about pursuing someone he shouldn't.

'So, we're *both* sad and lonely people,' she said.

'I thought you weren't a pessimist?' he argued.

He didn't plan on being sad or lonely tonight. He planned on going out. Meeting up with a couple of the younger guys from uni. Seeing how everyone else's first shifts had gone. Drinking a few beers, maybe. Not too many. Meeting a nice girl… Someone available. Someone temporary. Someone to have a laugh with.

He wouldn't have a late night. He wouldn't be a naughty boy. He was on an early shift with Sophie tomorrow morning and needed to be at the station for seven a.m.

Sophie shook her head, still smiling, and he began to wonder if this was just a mask she put on at work.

'I'm not. Not really,' she said.

Suddenly he wanted to discard his plans for the night and suggest to Sophie that she join him. They could go out to a decent gastro pub or something. Grab a bite to eat, get to know each other a bit more...

Only he didn't. This was his first day, and she was his mentor, and she was heavily pregnant and he didn't need to involve himself with her life or her problems. He needed to maintain a distance. This was professional between them. Her being pregnant and single screamed issues.

'Good. Well...thanks for today. It was great. I'll see you tomorrow morning.'

'Yes. Thanks, Theo. You did well.'

He nodded. 'You too.'

He raised a hand and began to walk away, realising as he did so that he really didn't want to go. Something about Sophie made him want to stay. To talk to her a bit more. Learn a bit more about her.

Why was she alone? Where was the father of her child? What had happened?

Questions that he really ought not to ask on the first day of meeting her, but questions he somehow wanted answers to.

But Sophie was not his problem. She was his mentor. Nothing else. He needed to put her out of his mind.

They hadn't had much opportunity to talk today. The shift had been pretty full-on and most of their chat had been about the calls themselves, the patients, the trust policy and the like. Only occasionally had they ventured into personal territory, and even then it had been pretty light, such as the conversation about his sisters and their pregnancy cravings.

He hoped to talk to her a bit more tomorrow. Make it clear that he was not only interested in the job, but in her as a person, too. That he was a nice guy.

By the time he got home he still hadn't shifted the feeling that he'd wanted to stay with her, and all he could think about was the way her face looked when she talked about her cases. The way she sometimes tucked her hair behind her ears when she was concentrating on her driving. The way she tilted her head when she looked at him, as if she were curious and intrigued about him, too.

He liked that. The fact that she didn't make him feel like just another student. That she saw him as a person.

He had to admit that if he'd met her in a pub, or a club, he would most certainly have asked her out. If she wasn't pregnant, of course! Clearly she had something going on there, and he didn't want to get mixed up in whatever was going on with the father, but...

There was something about Sophie.

He couldn't put his finger on it. Couldn't

name whatever it was. He just knew that he had to know more about the woman he was going to be spending his days with.

Theo woke before his alarm the next morning and got up quickly, feeling eager to get to his morning shift with Sophie.

He'd spent a weird night out with his friends. He'd been surrounded by people he liked, sharing a drink or playing a game of pool on one of the pub's tables when one came free, but he hadn't felt *present* in their company.

His mind had been elsewhere.

At one point he must have been staring into space, because his friend Marty had given him a nudge and asked him if he was okay.

'Yeah, sure! Just thinking about today. Processing it, you know...'

'You sure you weren't thinking about Sophie?'

He'd blinked. Laughed. 'Why would I be thinking about her?'

'I was at the same station as you, mate. I saw her with my own eyes, you lucky so-and-so! My mentor isn't as pretty to look at, with his frizzy hair and his beer belly. You've hit the jackpot, mate.'

Theo had taken a sip of his beer. 'It's not

like that. Besides, she's pregnant. She's with someone.'

Marty had simply raised his eyebrows. 'That's not what my guy says.'

He and Marty had talked about her? 'What did your guy say?' He'd been intrigued.

'That she got dumped. That she's really hung up on the father and a bit of a cold fish.'

Theo had dismissed that. 'Sounds like she once turned your guy down and he's just bitter. She's not like that. She's really nice.'

He and Marty hadn't spoken any more about their mentors after that, choosing instead to discuss the cases they'd seen and what they'd been allowed to do. But all night he'd pondered on what Marty had said about Sophie being hung up on her baby's father.

Was she pining for him? Hoping he'd come back to her? And why did it irritate Theo that some of the others had been talking about her behind her back? She was really nice—she didn't deserve that. Especially if some bloke had dropped her like a hot rock, leaving her with a child to look after.

He took a shower and got ready, then drove his car to the ambulance station, grabbing some breakfast from a petrol station on the way. Whilst there, he picked up a packet of red liquorice without really thinking about it, and walked into the station to find Sophie already by the car, about to work through the checklist.

'Morning, Theo.'

'Morning. Want me to do that?'

'You remember how to do it?'

'I do.'

'Knock yourself out.'

She smiled at him and he smiled back, careful not to let her happy face mean too much to him. He wasn't here to make Sophie happy. Not in that way, anyway. He was here to get an education. Get through his placement and move on.

He reminded himself of the first items on the clipboard and checked the stock, signing with his initials and dating everything, noting that Sophie had now opened the bonnet and was checking the oil and then, afterwards, the tyres and the lights.

It took them just a few moments, working together.

He closed the boot. 'All present and correct.'

She smiled. 'Good. Checked the oxygen tanks?'

'Two full tanks and one that's three-quarters full.'

'Perfect.'

He slid into the passenger seat and put on his seat belt, before pulling his little gift from his shirt pocket. 'I got you this.' He passed her the red liquorice, feeling a bit awkward.

'Oh!' She laughed. 'You didn't have to do that! That's so sweet of you.'

'It wasn't a problem.'

She put the liquorice into the compartment that sat between them. 'I'll have that later. Right! Are you ready?'

'Yep.'

'Good. You can call in to Control and get us rolling.'

He liked it that she was letting him do things, and he was pleased that he'd made himself remember their call number. He picked up the radio. 'Control, this is six zero two. We're clear and ready for calls.'

'Thanks, six zero two. Have a good shift.'

'You too.'

He put the radio down and smiled at Sophie as she started the engine and rolled out of the ambulance station. He had a good feeling about today. At that moment he felt as if nothing in the world could ruin his good mood.

He had no idea that their first patient— or rather their first patient's relative—would change all that.

They'd been on duty for over twenty minutes before their first shout came through from Control. An elderly woman in her eighties having breathing difficulties, a known COPD patient.

Sophie hit the lights and sirens as they drove quickly to the address in Kingston upon Thames. As always, her mind raced ahead to the possibilities of what she might need to do when attending her patient.

'Do you know about COPD?' she asked Theo.

'Chronic Obstructive Pulmonary Disease.'

'But do you know what that actually means?'

'Patients with COPD have difficulty with their breathing and oxygenating properly.'

'Good. But we can't be railroaded into thinking that just because this patient has COPD, this is a respiratory issue. The patient's age means this could also be cardiac, and we need to think about possible comorbidities—medical conditions that usually occur at the same time as another condition,' she explained.

Theo nodded. 'But treatment would be to give her oxygen, right?'

'Once we've checked her SATs and found out her usual range of oxygenation. We don't give COPD patients full-flow oxygen because of oxygen toxicity. It causes them to retain carbon dioxide, so we need to maintain a low pressure of oxygen in the blood. We give them just enough oxygen to keep their usual levels of saturation, which is generally between eighty-eight and ninety-two per cent in a COPD patient. The oxygen canisters flow at fifteen litres on full, so with this patient we'll start at two litres and see how she goes. When we get there you can put the SATs monitor on her finger and get out the oxygen and an adult mask. You remember how to attach them?'

Theo nodded.

She had confidence that he understood all the risks. He'd been invaluable yesterday. Calm, assured. He had shown no sign of panic at any of the calls they'd attended, and had kept family members reassured. She had no doubt that he would follow her instructions to the letter.

They entered the outskirts of Kingston and the traffic pulled over to get out of their way as they headed down a small close, pulling up outside their patient's home. It was a narrow, terraced house, neat and tidy, with a front garden filled with pots and a newly painted front door.

Theo helped her carry the equipment out, and before she could knock on the door it was opened by a young woman. 'Come in, come in. It's my nan. She's…' The woman looked past Sophie and noticed who she was with. *'Theo?'*

Theo looked startled, and Sophie knew a whole lot of words and thoughts and feelings were not being made clear as the two looked at each other. The young woman looked shocked, and Theo didn't look very happy at all...*uncomfortable*.

But if there was anything these two needed to say to each other they'd have to do it later. There was an elderly lady here who needed help. And, although Sophie felt sure that there had been something between Theo and the young woman, she went to move inside the house.

She frowned as the other woman just stood there, blocking the way, still staring at her student. She turned to look at Theo and noticed a look of grim determination on his face. *Enough!* If these two had a history they could sort it later.

'Could you show us where your nan is? Is she upstairs?'

The young woman nodded, finally stepping aside to let them pass.

Sophie hurried up the stairs, trying to ignore the way her baby had suddenly started kicking violently in her belly. It was as if she was trying to kick down the walls of her confinement. She had to push her hand down hard, just beneath her ribs, to get the baby to stop for a moment. She didn't need this. Her patient was what mattered here. But for some reason all she could think about was how Theo and this woman knew each other. Friends? Romantically involved?

None of my damned business.

Sophie turned into a lavender-painted bedroom to find an elderly woman sitting up in bed, her chest making huge movements as she tried to breathe in air. She looked quite pale, and was most definitely breathless. The young woman behind her—the one who knew Theo—had done the right thing in calling for help.

Sophie smiled at the old lady, laying her jump bag down on the floor. 'Hello, my lovely, my name's Sophie and I'm a paramedic. I've got Theo with me, and he's a student. Can you tell me your name?'

Sophie glanced behind her at Theo, to tell him that she would need the SATs probe, but he was already kneeling down, unzipping the bag to get it out for her.

'Diana… Dodsworth…' the elderly lady breathed.

'And how long have you been like this, Diana?'

Sophie watched as Theo slipped the probe onto Diana's finger. It took just a moment to show that Diana's oxygen levels were at eighty-four percent.

Can you get the oxygen? she mouthed to Theo, but he was already on it.

'Your oxygen levels are a little low,' she told her patient. 'Do you know what you usually run at?'

'About ninety,' said the young woman, leaning against the door.

'Thank you. And what's your name?'

The young woman glanced at Theo. 'Jen.'

'Any other medical conditions I should know about?' she asked Jen as she helped put the oxygen mask over Diana's face and turned on the flow at a low level.

'Type two diabetes. High blood pressure and emphysema.'

'All right.' She turned back to Diana and laid her hand on the patient's. 'You just take nice steady breaths for me, okay? Any chest pain?'

'A little.'

'Okay. We'll set up for an ECG, just to be on the safe side. Theo, can you pass me the electrodes?'

She set about placing the electrodes discreetly on Diana's chest, wrists and legs, and told her to lie still whilst the ECG machine took a reading. Sophie tore off the strip of paper and scanned it carefully. Normal sinus rhythm, which was good. This was most definitely an exacerbation of a respiratory issue. A flare-up of emphysema, which was a long-term progressive disease of the lungs. It caused shortness of breath due to the alveoli in the lungs becoming over-inflated and damaged and therefore unable to work properly.

'I'm just going to take your blood sugar level,' she told Diana.

Theo was already passing her what she needed.

Two days in and he was working well with her. Knowing the way she worked, what she would need next, ready to pass it to her. He was doing well as a student and she was impressed. Plus, he wasn't letting whatever was going on between him and Jen affect him.

Sophie cleaned Diana's finger and took a small sample of blood to analyse. It came back normal.

'And now your blood pressure...' She fastened the sphygmomanometer cuff around Diana's thin arm. 'Keep breathing for me. You'll feel this tighten around your arm, but it shouldn't hurt.'

Diana's blood pressure came back slightly raised, and her pulse was fast, but that was to be expected, considering the fact that she couldn't breathe very well and was probably afraid. It was terrifying to have to call out an ambulance. Nobody wanted to go to hospital.

Sophie checked her patient's oxygen levels. The low-flow oxygen was helping, bringing

Diana's levels back to nearly ninety per cent. 'You're doing much better now, Diana. Nearly got you back to normal!'

'I didn't expect to see you again, Theo,' said Jen suddenly.

Sophie turned to look at the young woman, then glanced at Theo.

'No.'

A man of few words.

'How do you two know each other?' Sophie asked, feeling intrigued now that her patient was stable.

'He was my boyfriend,' Jen said, looking at Theo with what looked like some unresolved anger. 'Now he's my ex.'

Intriguing, all right. But still not my business.

Sophie looked back at Diana. 'Well, my lovely, you've got a decision to make. When the ambulance gets here you can decide if you want to go in to be checked at the hospital or stay at home. It's totally up to you. I've got your levels back to normal, but we'll need to see what happens when we take you off the oxygen. Shall we try to do that?'

Diana nodded and removed the mask as Sophie turned the nozzle on the oxygen cannister to zero.

'Just sit and breathe normally. I'll leave the

SATs probe on your finger and we'll see how you do.'

'Okay.'

Sophie turned back to look at Theo. 'So why did you two break up?'

Curiosity had got the better of her. Theo was stunning, and he seemed kind and hard-working and considerate. He listened to her when she talked, and he appeared to be empathetic. He'd been in the army, for crying out loud! And Jen appeared to be the very type she'd imagined Theo going out with. Young, slim, curves to die for... The kind of woman who took three hours to do her hair and make-up before leaving the house and who ought to have shares in fake tan.

Unlike me. Most definitely unlike me, Sophie thought. *I think getting ready to go out takes ten minutes. A quick brush of my hair, a bit of mascara, some lip balm and—boom! I'm out the door.*

Jen gave a short laugh, but there was no humour in it. 'Because Theo runs at the first sign of commitment. One hint that I wanted to talk about us getting serious and he disappeared from my life faster than a bank robber in a getaway car.'

Theo shook his head, as if silently disagreeing, but said nothing.

Sophie looked at him curiously. A commitment-phobe, huh? Well, she knew the type. All too well. She'd known there had to be *something* wrong with him. And unfortunately, men like him were *not* in short supply. It was disappointing. She'd been beginning to think that Theo might be different from Connor.

Never mind. I'll get over it.

Outside, Sophie heard the tell-tale engine sounds of the ambulance arriving. She glanced at Diana's SATs. 'Your levels keep dropping, Diana, so my advice to you is to go into hospital, but it's your choice.' She placed the oxygen mask back onto her patient's face and turned the flow on. 'Could you let the other paramedics in?' she asked Jen.

Jen turned and hurried down the stairs.

Sophie glanced at Theo and raised an eyebrow. He passed her the keypad to finish off inputting the details that he hadn't been shown how to do.

'I think… I'd better go in… I'm on my own here… Jen only visits when…she can.' Diana glanced at Theo. 'You broke her heart, you know.'

Theo looked sorry.

The thud of footsteps coming up the stairs told Sophie that the cavalry had arrived, and she stood up, groaning at the stiffness in her knees, before handing over to the ambulance crew. Josh and Sam were a good pair. She had no doubt that they would look after her patient very well and have her laughing and smiling by the time they pulled up outside the hospital.

Sophie and Theo stayed whilst Diana was wrapped up, strapped into a carry-chair and taken outside to the ambulance. Jen clambered in with her after locking up the house, and the ambulance pulled away after switching one of Sophie's empty oxygen cannisters with one of their full ones from the store they kept on board.

She didn't mean to poke her nose into Theo's business, but the question just came out… 'So, what happened there, then? Between you and Jen? She seemed quite bitter.'

'We just weren't right for each other. We wanted different things.'

'Like what?'

He shrugged. 'I think she saw more of a future for us than I did.'

'You weren't looking for a future?'

He sighed as he helped store the bags away and closed the boot of their vehicle. 'She wanted to move our relationship on a lot quicker than I did. We'd been going out for just a couple of months. I thought it was just casual fun, but she started talking about wanting me to meet her parents. About moving in and getting a cat.'

'A cat?'

They got into the car and pulled on their seat-belts.

'A rescue cat. She had this idea that we should go to a rehoming centre and pick the oldest, mangiest cat they had and give it a new life.'

'And…you don't like cats?'

'Cats are fine. Rescuing a cat is even finer. But how could we give one a stable home when I didn't even think *we* were stable? She wanted to show the world how happy we were. But I wasn't in the same place. I thought she was just someone I was having fun with when I had free time. I didn't see a future between us. I thought I'd made my feelings clear from the start. So, we had all these arguments… I kept trying to pull away and she kept holding on. She pushed for too much and I wasn't ready.'

'So, she was moving faster than you?'

He nodded. 'I just wasn't the right person for Jen, and she's bitter about it because all her friends have settled down and she's still single.'

Sophie nodded, considering for a moment. Then she called through to Control and made them aware that they were clear of their last job. 'Do you think you'll ever settle down with someone, some day?'

Theo bristled and shook his head. 'If I'm honest? No. I like my life as it is right now. Uncomplicated and free. I don't need anyone else to worry about.'

He sounded terse. But what right did she have to be upset by that? She barely knew Theo. She understood what had been driving Jen, though. The pursuit of happiness. The dream. Lots of little girls grew up reading about princesses and their magical love stories, how one day their prince would come. And when everyone around you seemed to be settling down and finding that happiness you so desperately sought yourself… Well, it did things to you. It made you hungry for what you wanted and sometimes you made poor choices in trying to find it. Attached yourself to the wrong type of people.

Jen had done so. As had Sophie.

But people were entitled to want different things. Not everybody could want the same destination in life.

She'd thought Connor wanted the same things as her. But she'd discovered much too late that they'd had different dreams about the future. Here she was, towards the end of her pregnancy, looking forward to being a mother and settling down, raising her child in a home full of love, and yet Theo, who was roughly the same age, wanted the exact opposite. A life of freedom where the only person he had to look after was himself.

Was that selfish of him? Or wise? Because every time she'd got involved with someone it had led to heartbreak. *Her* heartbreak. She'd not even been able to rely on her parents, and they were the two people in the whole wide world a person should be able to trust the most. If they could let you down, why wouldn't everyone else?

'Good for you,' she said now, as if she understood. But to be truly honest she didn't—not really. All Sophie wanted was to be loved. Unconditionally. And she wanted to love someone back with a love that was so deep and so passionate. She wanted to share her life with someone who would make her laugh and smile and cry…someone who would move her…someone who would hold her and comfort her and protect her.

Theo wanted none of that. But what pleasure was there in a life lived alone?

Angrily she ripped open the packet of red liquorice that Theo had bought her and took a huge bite of one long string. The sweetness, the taste, was a loving caress within her mouth, and made her feel a little bit better. But as she drove away from Diana's house, she tried to decipher why Theo's life choices should make her feel so unsettled…

CHAPTER THREE

THEO STOOD UNDER the shower, letting the hot water hit his face and run down his body. It had been a long day, which had gone wrong the moment they'd attended that first shout, where they'd found Jen—his ex-girlfriend.

He'd tried to be polite when talking about her to Sophie. He hadn't wanted to come across as someone who told tales when the other person wasn't around to defend themselves, but somehow, since that call, he'd sensed that Sophie seemed a little different. A bit brusquer in her dealings with him. A bit more tense. Less willing to crack a joke with him.

They'd attended a call to a fire, where it had been reported there was someone still stuck in a house. That had turned out to be untrue, but they'd waited at a safe distance as the fire brigade had put out the flames and he'd tried to engage Sophie in conversation.

'Do you get called to many fires?' he'd asked.

'Some.'

Sophie had been looking at the house, chewing on her liquorice, watching the flames as they rose higher out of the hole in the roof where part of it had collapsed. All around it the fire officers had been working frantically, hoses positioned strategically.

'I guess you've seen some terrible things?'

'It's part of the job.'

She had been abrupt. Brisk. Still not looking at him.

He had started to feel he'd done something wrong and had tried to work out what. Had it been something to do with meeting Jen? Was Sophie angry at the way he'd treated her? Spoken about her? Why? Was it a female thing?

'I guess you have to learn coping strategies to deal with the stress,' he'd said.

She'd said nothing for a moment. Then, 'You can ask for counselling if you need it.'

'Have *you* ever needed it?'

She'd looked at him then. Shaken her head. Chewed her liquorice. 'No.'

Plumes of grey-black smoke had billowed into the sky overhead, turning everything grey. The whole street had come out to watch the fire, huddling their loved ones closer to each other behind the safety lines taped up by the fire crew.

Theo had watched their faces. Seen the relief, the gratitude that it wasn't them that this had happened to, and also the guilt at feeling such gratitude, the curiosity and the need to see the terrible thing that was happening.

Sophie had been dumped, Marty had said. But she hadn't mentioned the father of her child once. In fact, she'd barely told him anything about herself except for the fact that she lived alone. He could be totally barking up the wrong tree, but what if she felt that she'd once tried to give everything to a prospective romance, but the guy hadn't? She'd said she lived alone, but what did that actually mean?

'Do you have someone? Someone special?' he'd asked, glancing once more at the families behind them, as if thinking of them.

Sophie had pursed her lips as if considering her answer. 'Depends what you mean by "special".'

'What about the father of your baby?'

Sophie finally turned to look at him and gave him a wry look. 'He wasn't ready for commitment. He wanted to be free from responsibility. Said it would be all too much for him, having a child. That he still felt like a child himself. He couldn't *wait* to get away from me. Good riddance, I say. Best I found out sooner, rather than later.'

So, he had guessed right. He'd left Jen when she'd wanted more and the baby's father had left Sophie when *she'd* wanted more. Needed more from him. She felt abandoned and she probably figured Theo to be the same kind of man.

But he didn't feel the same as this other man. He couldn't imagine he'd be so irresponsible as to get a woman pregnant and then walk away! He didn't particularly *want* the responsibility of a child, but if he made one then he'd damn well do the right thing! Whoever the father of Sophie's baby was, he was a different kind of man entirely, and Theo definitely felt they couldn't be compared. Their situations were different.

But he hadn't known how to say that there and then, as they'd watched the fire. Sophie was obviously still hurting, no matter how much she pretended she was fine, and he'd wondered how raw the pain was.

Pregnancies lasted nine months, if they were carried to full term, and if Sophie had found out about the pregnancy when she was around two months, then the father of her child had only recently left her. Within the last year. Was she getting more and more scared as the birth loomed? Had she imagined having someone to hold her hand as she went into labour? The father?

Now she knew she would have to face labour and the birth alone. Raise a child alone. And what about her career? It was going to be difficult for her to juggle the two. He didn't know her very well, but from what he did know, he thought she'd give it her all.

The water felt good on his neck and shoulders as he turned under the spray, and he allowed it to pound down on the tense muscles in his back too.

He hadn't known what to say to Sophie to reassure her that he was nothing like her baby's father. That even though he wasn't a man who sought out responsibility, who wanted his life to remain free and unencumbered by complicated relationships and burdens, he was still a good guy. Honourable and kind and trustworthy.

Perhaps if I can't tell her, I can show her.

He would show her what a good guy he was. That even though he was a man who didn't want to settle down yet, she could still depend on him. That he could be there for her—not just as her student, but as a great colleague and an amazing friend.

Relationships between a man and a woman didn't all have to be about sex or love. He liked her. *Really* liked her. It wouldn't be hard at all. And, even though he thought she was an incredibly attractive woman, the romantic element wouldn't be a problem because he would never get involved with her in that way.

She was about to be a mother. A single mother. All they could have together was friendship.

Sophie woke still feeling tired after a difficult disturbed night's sleep. The baby had tossed and turned for hours, poking and prodding at her internal organs—more often than not her bladder, meaning she'd had to keep getting up and going for a wee. It was as if the baby was testing her perimeter for weaknesses.

'You'll find your way out one day. Just not yet, okay?' she said as she rubbed at her abdomen and yawned.

Getting out of bed proved to be a bit of a problem. Her pelvis really ached, especially down low at the front, so she took things slowly as she headed downstairs to get breakfast.

In the kitchen, she grabbed some juice and some cereal and, not for the first time, noticed Connor's favourite bowl, still sitting at the bottom of the stack at the back of the cupboard. He'd forgotten to take it when he left and she kept meaning to throw it out, but something made her keep it.

Why? He was hardly going to come back now, was he? He'd made it quite clear that a future with her and their baby was not the kind of future he'd envisaged for himself. Not yet, anyway.

'I do want kids, Soph, just not now! We're too young! I'm just getting started in my career!'

Nice to know that his job prospects came before she did. Before their *child* did.

Sophie was used to feeling second-best—even third-best, at times. She'd always been damned well determined that her own child would never feel that way—and what had happened? Connor had dumped them both. Her child wasn't even born yet, and he hadn't considered either of them important enough to remain on his radar.

His desertion had made her feel as if *she* was the one who had let her child down by not being able to keep its father. Not being good enough. But she was damned if he was going to make her feel that way.

Her daughter would see a strong mother. A resilient mother. Not one held back by the tragedy of a lost love the way her own mother had been.

Sophie's daughter would need her. Love her. Want her. Be proud of her. Rely on her.

Until she became a surly teenager, knowing her luck.

At least I'm good at my job. I help people. I

save lives. I make a difference. People might not want to stick around me, but I make them live another day if I can.

Whilst she waited for her kettle to boil she grabbed a piece of liquorice from the packet that Theo had bought her yesterday. It made her think of him. Of her reaction to him when he'd first walked into the ambulance station. The way he could make her laugh. The way he often made her smile. How hot he was, with that body, those perfect teeth, that hypnotic smile that just made her want to stare at him and stare at him until the trance was broken.

But the things Jen had said… The things *he'd* said… They had confirmed that he was just like Connor, only better-looking, which made it all the more disappointing, because those thoughts were like a bucket of ice.

Just once, would it hurt for her to come across a guy who didn't think of his own needs first? Someone selfless and giving and loving and trustworthy? Someone you could trust one hundred per cent to turn up and not let you down? Someone you just knew would be there for you no matter what?

Was it too much to ask?

She took her coffee upstairs, grimacing slightly at the ache in her pelvis as she climbed the stairs. What was that? Had she got out of bed wrong? Strained a muscle? She hoped it wasn't the beginning of that SPD thing she'd heard about… Symphisis pubis dysfunction was a condition caused by stiffness in the pelvic joints either at the front or the back. It wasn't harmful to the baby, but it could be incredibly painful for the mother, and make it difficult to get around.

She'd been doing fine up till now. She'd felt as fit as a fiddle. Some days she barely remembered she was pregnant until she got home and noticed her ankles beginning to swell, and then she'd sit with her feet up, watching a show on the television.

Sophie was loath to take painkillers. Besides, it was probably temporary anyway, and she needed to get dressed and get to work. Once there, she'd forget anyway, as her patients' needs and concerns always superseded her own.

It didn't take her long to get ready, and she was soon out of her house and on her way to the station. The sun was out in full force today, and she could tell it was going to be a really hot day. The sky was a beautiful azure blue, and totally cloudless, and she had a really pleasant drive to work, with her radio on, singing away.

As she pulled in, she saw Theo, and noticed her heart beat a little faster. How many times was that going to happen? When would her body get used to the sight of seeing him and calm the hell down?

She grabbed her bottle of water and saw him wave at her from across the car park, and then he began striding over.

'Okay, Sophie, play it cool,' she told herself, swinging her legs out of her car and trying to stand up.

The pain in her pelvis shot an ice pick through her and she knew she must have winced or gasped.

'Hey, you okay?' He was at her side in an instant, worry etched into his face as he grabbed her hand and arm, helping her stand straight.

Embarrassed, with her skin burning from his touch, his proximity, the way he seemed always to be there for her, she pulled herself free and took a step back. 'I'm fine! Honestly. Just a bit stiff today, that's all.'

'You're sure?'

'Of course I'm sure.'

He didn't look as if he totally believed her. But that was his problem. Not hers.

'Come on. We need to get a move on.' She pushed past him, trying to saunter casually into the station, but someone perhaps ought to have told her that an eight-and-a-half-months pregnant woman couldn't *saunter* anywhere.

He caught up with her and walked alongside. 'You looked like you were in pain. Were you having a contraction? Braxton Hicks?'

Sophie was irritated with herself for giving that impression, but she laughed it off. 'It was just a twinge.'

'My sisters all got twinges like that towards the end of their pregnancies. It's the body preparing itself for labour. But if you're having problems you need to tell your midwife—there are things they can suggest to help.'

She stopped in her tracks and faced him, amused, her hands on her child-bearing hips. 'Are you a fully-fledged paramedic?'

He looked directly at her, as if wondering where this was going. 'No, I'm not.'

'Are you a doctor?'

'No.'

'An actual midwife?'

He shook his head, smiling now. 'No.'

'Then you're not qualified to give me any advice. Now, I'm perfectly fine—so jump to it and complete those duty checks!'

He smiled at her as she started to walk away. He called after her. 'Are you an army major?'

Sophie stopped and turned. She raised her eyebrows, knowing the game was about to be played on her. She smiled. 'No.'

'A drill sergeant?'

'No.'

He saluted. 'You certainly sound like one.'

She couldn't help it. She imagined herself standing in front of a line of raw recruits, bellowing orders at them, telling them off for stepping out of line. And Theo looked so cute in his paramedic's uniform, saluting her as if she was his captain or something. She smirked. And when he laughed, she found herself laughing, too.

'I guess I asked for that. Honestly, Theo!' She gave him a gentle shove and he laughed again, playfully rubbed at his arm. 'You do make me smile.'

He laughed, his face full of warmth and kindness and charm. 'Good.'

And just for a moment she found herself staring at him, wondering what it might be like to kiss him. To have him hold her. Touch her.

What the hell am I doing?

She turned away, annoyed with herself. Because she'd begun to stare—and what was the point of that? The wishing? The hoping? Theo was like Connor. He didn't want commitment, he didn't need the burden of another man's child, and he most certainly was not interested in her!

* * *

They were just about to drive away from the station when one of the other paramedics, Ross, flagged them down.

'Hey, guys. Just wanted to give you a reminder about tonight. The Wheatsheaf? Seven-thirty?'

Sophie frowned, then realisation dawned. 'Of course! Your thirtieth birthday party. Don't worry, I hadn't forgotten.'

Ross smiled at her. 'No, of course not. I'm sure baby brain isn't a real thing. Why don't you come along, Theo? The more the merrier.'

Theo was happy to be included in the celebrations. 'That'd be great. Sure!'

Sophie turned to him. 'Oh, you don't have to if you don't want to. I know you've probably got assignments and essays to write for uni.'

'You make it sound like you don't want me there. I can take a night off.' He leaned forward, past Sophie, to shake Ross's hand. 'I'll see you there.'

Ross nodded and began walking away.

Theo glanced across at Sophie. 'Will you need a lift? I'd be happy to pick you up and take you home again.'

She shook her head. 'You don't have to do that. You'll want to enjoy yourself, and if you're driving you can't have a drink.'

Was it her nature to push all men away, or just him? He'd hate to think it was only him having this effect on her.

'That's okay. I don't need to drink to have fun. It's no problem. Let me pick you up. I think you mentioned you live in Berrylands, right? It's on my way to The Wheatsheaf—it makes practical sense.'

'Oh…well…um…thanks. That's very practical of you.'

'No problem. Ready to go?'

She stared back at him. 'I am.'

He watched as she picked up the radio and told Control that they were ready for duty.

'That's great, six zero two. We have a job that's just come in. Sounds like a hypoglycaemic attack. Thirty-one-year-old woman. Flat Eight, Paradise Heights, Ewell Road, Tolworth.'

'Show us as being on our way, Control. Six zero two out.'

'Blues and twos?' Theo asked.

She smiled. 'Hit the switch.'

He fastened his seatbelt as Sophie drove them out of the ambulance station. Once again, he marvelled at the powerful engine of the car as she roared down the A3, smoothly passing the vehicles that got out of their way. She showed a brief moment of irritation when someone in the fast lane didn't bother looking in their rear-view mirror and didn't get out of the way for a few seconds, but eventually the driver saw them, raised his hand in apology, and pulled into the middle lane to let them pass.

'Tell me what you know about hypoglycaemia,' Sophie said as she drove.

He racked his brain for facts. 'Er…low blood sugar…mainly affects diabetics.'

'Signs and symptoms?'

'Turning pale, sweating, shaking, fast heartbeat, confusion…patients could pass out.'

'How do we treat?'

'Try and get them to drink or eat something sugary. Test their blood sugar. Give oxygen if conscious?'

'And if they're unconscious?'

'Recovery position and monitor.'

'Good. You're doing well.'

'I've got a good teacher.'

She smiled at the compliment.

Ahead of them the Tolworth Tower loomed large. They weren't far away now.

As they pulled up outside Paradise Heights Theo got out of the car quickly and grabbed the jump bag, then waited for Sophie to get out. She was most definitely struggling a little today, and he wondered if maybe she ought to take it easy a little bit. She had to be very late in her pregnancy now. Why hadn't she stopped working? He was all for women working until they needed to stop, but surely she had to be feeling the effects of being so heavily pregnant? His sisters had used to get swollen ankles and back-ache and nausea if they'd tried to do too much.

There was a flight of stone steps up the side of the house to flat number eight. They both climbed it and a man opened the door as they reached the top.

'She's in here. I've given her a fizzy drink and a chocolate bar.'

They followed the man inside the dark flat and Theo quickly took in the shabbiness of the place. There were no proper curtains up at the window, just a stained sheet held by pegs to a curtain rail. No carpet to speak of, only a tatty rug in front of the electric fire that was fixed to the wall. The air was stale and musty.

On a torn couch a woman lay, half propped up by cushions, looking pale and shaky. 'I'm feeling a bit better, I think.'

'What's your name?' Sophie asked.

'Melanie.'

'And how old are you, Melanie?'

Theo already knew the answer. It had come in with the call description. Sophie must be checking that Melanie was thinking clearly. He'd heard that some diabetics could be quite muddled after losing consciousness.

'Thirty-one,' said Melanie.

'And what's the date?'

Melanie thought for a moment. 'I never know the date. Ask me another one.'

Sophie smiled. 'Who's the Prime Minister?'

The patient told them.

'Good. Now, I'm just going to let Theo check your blood sugar and your SATs for me, okay?'

'Okay.'

Theo was thrilled that Sophie was giving him an opportunity to do the assessments on the patient himself. It showed she trusted him, and he liked that.

It soon became clear that Melanie was doing much better and her levels were almost back to normal.

'I don't think there's any need to take you into hospital,' Sophie said. 'Are you usually good on your blood sugars?'

Melanie nodded. 'That's the one thing I am in control of. But my parents aren't very well. I spent all of last night there and I simply forgot to eat.'

'Well, you won't do that again, hopefully.'

The patient laughed. 'Definitely not! I don't want to feel that way again—it was horrible. Thank God I've got Simon here to look after me.'

When Theo and Sophie got back to the car,

Theo couldn't help but ask the question. 'You say you live alone, but you must have someone you can call to look after you? You know…like family? When you really need someone.'

Sophie looked awkward. 'Who do *you* have?'

'If I needed to call on someone, I have three younger sisters, all desperate to stick their noses into my private life.'

He looked at her expectantly. Surely she had *someone*? Surely she wasn't really alone? Or was she a private individual who didn't think she needed to share details of her life with her student?

'I have friends,' she said.

'Friends?' He pushed down the boot lid and went round to his side of the car to get inside.

Sophie didn't look at him as she pulled her seatbelt around her large pregnant abdomen.

'What about the baby's father?'

'What about him?'

'Well, surely, he must want to—?'

'Connor gave up every right to pretend that he's a responsible, reliable person when he walked away from us.'

Theo felt bad for upsetting her. 'I'm sorry. I shouldn't have pushed. I was just… Look, not all men are the same as him. You can rely on me, if that helps at all.'

Sophie laughed out loud, as if what he'd just

said was the most ridiculous thing she'd ever heard in her life. 'I thought you didn't want any responsibilities?'

Theo smarted. 'I'm not suggesting we move in together. I'm saying I can be someone who's good in a crisis. Someone you could call.'

And he was. He was proud of that fact. He'd stepped up to look after his sisters when they'd needed it. Protected them. Raised them. He'd stepped up in the army. Protected the men in his troop. And he was the kind of man who was always there for his friends if they needed it.

His relationship with Jen had been moving at warp speed when he'd only ever wanted some casual fun. He'd thought he'd made it clear to Jen at the beginning what he was prepared to give—but, like most of the girls he'd dated, she'd said she understood and then tried to change his mind. Change *him*.

Sophie shouldn't judge him over one relationship that had gone sour.

He wouldn't mind helping Sophie if she needed it. They were hardly going to be an item, and as a friend, he could be there for her if needed.

'You're my teacher. My friend. And you said you could call on your friends. I *am* reliable. If I wasn't, do you think I would turn up every day? If I was unreliable, don't you think

I would have dropped out of the army earlier? Given up on my paramedic degree? I know how to commit to people I'm friends with, and I'm not a cold-hearted bastard, no matter what you may think.'

The cynical smile dropped from her face and she grew serious. 'Theo, you don't have to prove anything to me. We'll be together a month—no more than that—and there'll be no need for us to keep in touch after you've finished your placement. I don't expect to, either. You'll forget me and get on with your life. Just as you want.'

Did he detect a strange tone in her words? Her lack of belief in him saddened him. He was nothing like Connor. No, he didn't want responsibilities—but he was nothing like the father of her baby.

Stubbornness made him add, 'I'd like us to keep in touch.'

She started the engine. 'Fine. But time will tell what you'll do, won't it?'

For some reason Theo was feeling inordinately irritated that she thought so little about his level of commitment.

I'm a good guy!

'You know what? I'm going to make you a bet.'

'A bet?' She raised an eyebrow.

'That I can be relied upon. That I can look out for you. That I can be there if you need me. That I'll stick around longer than this placement and, hell, even hold your hand in hospital as you give birth, if you want. Because that's what friends do.'

She laughed out loud. 'I don't think I want you by my side as I give birth!'

'Why not? I was with one of my sisters as she delivered little Leo. Not at the business end, I might add, but I was there. I'm not squeamish. I'm a good guy, Sophie. I'm not like—' He stopped himself from saying it.

'The father of my child?' She smiled as if she wanted to believe him but didn't. 'You'll never be able to do it,' she said, sounding quite sure of herself. 'I'm sure you're a good friend, but a guy like you doesn't want to hang around with a single mother who has a newborn baby in tow. Especially one that isn't his.'

'Wow... I had no idea you thought so little of me.'

She glanced at him, looking a little guilty about what she'd just said. 'All right, Mr Finch! I hereby take your ridiculous most-definitely-will-fail bet that you be my best friend for... let's say one year? That should be plenty of time for you to get fed up and leave me behind on my lonesome. Especially when there's a screaming baby attached to me and my house stinks of dirty nappies. You want me calling you in the dead of the night, crying because I can't get my baby to latch on and I don't know what else to do? You're on!'

That sounded terrifying. But it was too late to back out now. He'd made a big thing of this and she'd called him on it.

'Deal!' He held out his hand, determined to show that he was serious. He knew he couldn't fail. But he also knew that she thought he would.

Well, he was looking forward to proving her wrong.

He was going to be the best friend anyone could ever have.

Screaming newborn baby or not.

CHAPTER FOUR

NOTHING FITTED. NOTHING in her goddamned wardrobe fitted! How long had it been since she'd last been on a night out? Months. When she'd not been pregnant and had been able to fit into all those figure-hugging dresses that had caught Connor's eye in the first place.

His favourite had been the red one with the spaghetti straps. It had a side zip, and she could still remember the look on his face when he'd first seen her in it. In fact, he'd been unable to wait to get her out of it.

She distinctly remembered that passionate encounter at a friend's house! Whilst everyone else had celebrated Kim and Joe's first wedding anniversary downstairs, she and Connor had been making out—up against a wall, no less! It had been as if he couldn't get enough of her, and afterwards he'd not let go of her hand, chatting with the other guests and glancing at her with a secret smile.

Back then, he'd certainly had the ability to make her head spin. Connor had seemed exciting and full of drive. She should have realised that that drive she'd loved so much about him only applied to his dreams. He wanted the top job, the promotions, the parties, the sex with the prettiest girl. And she had been the prettiest girl. Until she'd got pregnant and suddenly Connor had begun to back away. Almost as if she'd horrified him. Terrified him?

She couldn't put that dress on tonight. It wouldn't fit. And even if she did try to squeeze into it, the look on Theo's face would be one of hilarity. He'd probably curl into a ball on the floor, laughing so much—because, hey, friends took the mickey out of each other, didn't they?

Sophie slid hanger after hanger from one side of her wardrobe to the other, looking for something that was suitable for her growing abdomen and also looked as if it was party wear.

Why didn't I think to go shopping?

As she got to her last few pieces of clothing Sophie's mood was truly beginning to sour at the prospect of turning up at the party in her stretchy leggings and a tee shirt. And then she spotted, on the last hanger, a bottle-green maxi dress that she'd forgotten all about.

Perfect!

In fact, it was so perfect, and so unexpected,

she almost cried in relief at finding it. Now she could look forward to going out tonight! To showing that she might be at the end of her pregnancy and look like a beached whale, but she could still pull off some style.

She took the dress out of her wardrobe, checking to make sure it was clean, and hung it up on the outside of her wardrobe door as she sat in front of the mirror and tried to decide what to do with her hair. She wanted to make it look as if she'd made an effort for Ross's birthday without going overboard and making all her colleagues think she was on a date with her hunk of a student.

Relationships between colleagues weren't frowned upon in the ambulance service. There were even one or two married couples who worked together that she knew. It was rather that relationships weren't...*encouraged*... And she most certainly didn't want to do any encouraging of her own. There was a line with Theo. One she'd drawn all by herself. And she was determined, no matter how attracted she was to him, not to step over it.

What was she going to do with Theo? He'd promised her support and reliability, but she knew he'd only made that promise so that he didn't lose face.

And she knew that if she'd not been about

to become a new mother, but had instead been a hot single woman whom Theo had asked to take to a party, she'd be going full war paint mode—shaved legs, painted nails, perfume, skin-tight dress, heels…

Fancy matching underwear…

She almost felt resentment that she wasn't that hot young single woman any more, because if she was then Theo would be just her type. The guy who looked amazing. The one she always fell for, even knowing it would end badly, because that was what happened to her all the time.

Men like Theo didn't stick around for women like Sophie. They left her. Like Connor had. Like her father had. And all the other men who had been in her life looking for some quick and simple fun.

Way to put a downer on the night, Soph.

Perhaps she should wear her hair up? A few sparkly clips… Nothing fancy. Something to make herself feel good. This didn't have to be about attracting a man—it could be about making herself feel amazing. And why shouldn't she?

She opened her make-up bag. She didn't normally wear it, but tonight she would.

Lipstick? A small bit of mascara? Oh! And a squirt of this perfume will do.

She took off her bathrobe and slipped into the dress. It felt so nice not to have any constriction around her waist. There was a small pair of kitten heels that would go well with the dress, so she put those on, and found a silver bracelet and a long, low necklace, too.

There. Do I pass muster? Effort made, but not too much... I want to have some dignity, don't I? This is a party, after all.

She twisted this way and that in front of her full-length mirror and had to admit she looked pretty good! For a pregnant heffalump, anyway.

The ring of her doorbell told her that Theo had arrived.

Theo. Her new support system.

Her heart sped up a little at the thought of him seeing her. At work it was okay. She could hide behind her uniform and not be seen as a woman. But this was different. They wouldn't be working together tonight, and their relationship had shifted into this new dynamic. This friendship.

Theo was funny, incredibly attractive and *single*. And he was taking her out—as a friend— to a party. They weren't attending a call, or an emergency. They would be chatting. Laughing. Sharing jokes.

Oh, please, God, don't let there be any dancing!

Sophie loved to dance. It made her happy.

But to do so with Theo...? She could handle being close to him when he sat next to her in the car as her student and he was learning, but tonight he would be her equal and the rules would be different.

The doorbell rang again.

I'd better answer it, or he might think I've gone without him.

Could she do that? Pretend not to be in? But what would the point of that be? He'd still find her at the party. She couldn't ignore this. She had to get her head together and calm down and just remember that he was fulfilling a bet. Nothing more. He'd be full of enthusiasm at the beginning, but he'd fall away as everyone else did—and, hey, that was fine. She was used to it. She would cope, as she always did.

So why did a small part of her hope so badly that he wouldn't?

What would her life look like with Theo permanently in it?

What if this bet truly worked out and he turned out to be the best friend she'd ever had?

Nah. Not possible. Think of what Jen said. Theo bails.

'I won't be a minute!' she called out. There. She'd let him know she was here. That she hadn't run out on him.

Why am I so nervous? It's just Theo! He's nothing to me. This isn't a date.

That didn't help. In fact she just felt more nervous.

There was nothing else to do but open the door and let him in. She would just open it and pretend to look for something in her handbag. Not actually make eye contact, pretend the evening was nothing... She'd walk away from him and fetch her mobile from the kitchen counter top, and then he wouldn't compliment her, or fib about how beautiful she looked. She would try to ignore, or derail, all that awkward stuff.

Because, let's face it, I'll be coming home alone tonight.

Sophie walked towards the door, fully intending to act casual. But as she got closer to the door her nerves really kicked in and the baby began kicking too.

She placed a quivering hand on her belly and pulled the door open.

Theo stood there, looking so incredibly handsome and model-like in dark jeans and a fitted black shirt that he almost took her breath away. It wasn't right that a man should look so beautiful. So attractive. So edible.

'Wow! You look...' He seemed lost for words, too. 'Beautiful!'

Sophie blushed, hoping it was just her cheeks

colouring and not her neck and chest going
blotchy. Something about his reaction really
pleased her. She might feel as if she was the
size of an elephant, and she had begun, on occasion, to waddle like a duck, but it was thrill-
ing to discover that a handsome man like Theo
thought she looked beautiful—no matter how
many animals she thought she resembled.

Of course he could be lying, but…she'd take
the compliment anyway.

'Thanks. That's very sweet of you. You scrub
up quite well yourself.'

From behind his back, he pulled a perfectly
pink single rose. 'This is for you.'

A flower? She hadn't expected that. She
lifted the bloom to her nose and it smelt heavenly. But she had to force herself to remember
that this wasn't a romantic overture. He probably felt he couldn't turn up at her door empty-
handed. It was just a thing. A token. It didn't
mean anything.

'I'll put that in water.'

She took it through to the kitchen, aware that
her heart was racing like mad as she fiddled
with a small bud vase, trying her hardest not
to be clumsy and smash it all over the floor.
She filled the vase and added the rose, then
collected her handbag and went back to the
front door.

Theo still stood there, smiling, and he held out his arm for her to slip hers into. 'Shall we?'

Sophie smiled. 'Let's go.'

Why the hell did I let my pride force me into that stupid bet?

Sophie looked stunning. Simply stunning. Wholesome. Womanly. Full of curves. Her dress emphasised many pleasing features—the length of her neck, her delicate shoulder bones, an enticing décolletage—but most of all it enhanced the colour of her eyes, the way she looked at him. Demure. Nervous. With a shy smile.

That smile was *everything*.

The bloom of her belly beneath the dress had not sent him running in the other direction, as he suspected he would if he'd met her in a club or somewhere. Her pregnancy had seemed to draw him in. Draw him towards her, accelerating his desire to protect her and claim her.

He'd had to fight the yearning to move closer, to feel her baby bump against him, draw her lips to his…

Instead he'd presented her with the rose that he'd almost not brought in case she misconstrued it as something else.

They were hardly going on a date, and he'd made it quite clear that he wasn't a guy looking to get into a relationship. But, seeing how amazing she looked, feeling how much he suddenly wanted her, he was afraid for the first time since meeting her. So far his relationships with women had started well, but they always went sour when the women realised he didn't want to progress things as they did. And Sophie was a prime example of a woman who would want to progress things.

She was pregnant. About to be a mother. If she was looking for a man, she would be looking for someone to be a permanent fixture in her life and her baby's, and that wasn't the future for him.

He'd done all that. He'd taken on the responsibility for children who weren't his own—his sisters. When his father had abandoned them… when their mother had got sick. He'd become the man of the house, he'd looked after everyone, he'd kept them safe, fed them, clothed them. He didn't want to do that again. Because at the end of the day even his sisters had left him. Flown the nest, found men of their own, started families, leaving him behind.

He told himself that this was what he wanted. Freedom. And besides, Sophie had made it clear herself that there was to be a distance between them. She showed no signs of being attracted to him. Well, no overt ones. He'd caught her stealing glances at him when she'd thought he wasn't looking. Caught her considering him… sizing him up, almost. He was used to women looking at him. He knew they found him attractive. But relationships were built on more than looks, and neither of them wanted to progress something here.

Giving her the rose had given him time to recover as she'd turned to take it inside, and he'd stood there on her doorstep, sucking in some deep breaths and having a quiet word with himself as she found a vase.

Get a grip, man. Seriously.

By the time she returned, he'd plastered on a confident smile, and he offered her his arm and walked her out to his car—which he'd had cleaned after his shift.

He walked her to the passenger door and, like a gentleman, opened it for her.

'Thanks.'

'My pleasure.' He walked round to his side of the vehicle, trying to steady his breathing.

Normally Sophie was in the driving seat.

Tonight would be different.

The radio was playing some nice songs and the windows were down for their short drive in this summer evening to The Wheatsheaf, where Ross was holding his thirtieth birthday party. Theo managed to find a space in the car park and pulled into it.

'Stay there,' he said, getting out and going around to the passenger door and opening it. He held out his hand. 'My lady.'

Sophie laughed. 'Thank you, kind sir.'

It felt good, even if for that brief moment, to have her hand in his. But once she was standing and had gathered her bag he let go and walked with her into a private room at the pub, where they were greeted and cheered by a large group of off-duty paramedics who'd already had one or two drinks, by the sound of things.

They went over to the bar. 'What would you like to drink?' he asked.

'Oh, that's okay. I can buy my own.'

'Let me get these first ones.'

She nodded. 'All right, thank you. A fresh orange juice with lemonade, please.'

'Coming right up.'

He ordered two, as he was driving, and then they went to find a seat with their colleagues and friends, before heading over to the small buffet, where they could get sandwiches and sausage rolls and crisps.

It was a good crowd. Raucous. Loud. Full of tall tales and laughter. Music played in the far corner, where a DJ was mixing some tunes and people were dancing. One or two of their colleagues were discussing shouts they'd been on years ago, stories full of humour and disbelief at what some people got up to in the name of fun.

He found his gaze often drawn to Sophie. To the play of lights across her face, the way she laughed, the way she told stories of her own.

'I got called once to a man who had had an epileptic fit in an amusement arcade. I was working with another paramedic, on an ambulance, and we drove there like bats out of hell as an update on the call had come through, saying that the man was unconscious on the floor. Well, we got there, and found him lying on the carpet next to the one-armed bandits. He was just coming to. But next to him was this woman playing the slots. We asked her if she'd seen what had happened and she said she had—because she was his wife! She told us that he was sensitive to flashing lights and would come round eventually. So, we crouch down and get him sitting up, and as we do some coins fall out of his pocket. I scooped them up and passed them to his wife for safekeeping, and she thanked me and fed them straight into the machines! Seriously! If you know your husband is a photo-sensitive epileptic, then why take him to an arcade? It's ridiculous!'

And so the evening went on, with each paramedic trying to outdo the other with tales from work.

Theo found himself laughing and enjoying himself, but the thing he liked the most was the way Sophie would keep turning to look at him and they would smile at each other as if…

As if what?

Each time she looked at him like that he felt something he couldn't define. It was confusing.

But then everyone decided to get up and dance before the night was over and he found himself holding out his hand to her. 'One dance can't hurt.'

'I'd love to. But I weigh half a ton! It'll probably be safer for your toes if I stay sitting down.'

'I survived a car running over my foot once. I'm sure we'll be fine. Come on!' And he took her hand and escorted her to the dance floor.

There was a fun number on, but he kept it low-energy, holding her hand and slowly twirling her round now and then, like a ballerina in a jewellery box. Then he pulled her towards him and they danced together, until the DJ announced that they were going to end the night with something slow.

That wasn't their jam. They were friends. They didn't need to slow-dance together.

But he felt awkward about walking her back

to her seat. That would seem dismissive. So he decided to ignore all his loud, screaming thoughts, telling him to stop what he was doing right now, and he took Sophie's hand in his and laid his other hand on the small of her back.

He could feel her baby belly pressed up against him as they swayed in time with the music. He felt tense. Too aware of how close she was. How good she smelt. Her perfume was heavenly. Not overpowering, but light and floral.

He made himself relax. It was just a dance. A way to end the evening. He smiled at a sensation against his stomach. 'I can feel your daughter kicking me. Do you think she's telling me to back off?'

Sophie rested her head upon his shoulder. 'Maybe. Or she could just be telling me she wants something decent to eat.'

The buffet that the pub had provided was practically all gone. 'I could get you a bag of pork scratchings,' Theo said, 'but she'd probably be better having something more substantial.'

'I'd kill for some fish and chips.'

'You're really hungry?'

'I'm starving.'

That was it. His gentlemanly instincts kicked

in. 'If we go now, we can pick up some proper food on the way home—before they close.'

She nodded. 'Sounds good.'

'Come on, then.'

He kept her hand in his, almost without thinking about it, as he led her off the dance floor. They said their goodbyes to Ross and the rest of the team, citing the excuse that pregnant feet needed to rest and saying that they hoped he'd had a good birthday.

Theo tried to ignore the cheers and catcalls they received as they walked away together, but both of them were laughing as they emerged into the cooler night air.

'What are they like, huh?'

He opened the door for her once again, waiting for her to be safe inside the vehicle before getting in and driving them to a local fish and chip shop. He bought them both food and they sat in the car, eating with tiny wooden forks.

'Oh, my God, this is just so good!' said Sophie, closing her eyes in ecstasy.

The aroma in the car was one of salt and vinegar, but he had to admit it was very good. Just what he'd needed after a few hours of nothing but orange juice and some snacks.

'Agreed. Baby happy?'

'Mmm!' She laughed and popped another chip into her mouth.

He'd had a good night. It was funny, really. He spent ages pursuing fun and excitement with his friends—rock-climbing, white water rafting, paintballing, going to clubs—but the simplest of pleasures could come from the simplest of things. Good food with a friend who made him smile. He didn't do that enough.

He couldn't remember the last time he'd just sat and had a takeaway with a woman. He'd certainly never done it with Jen, who had only considered food worthy if it was presented well in a five-star restaurant and would look good with perfect lighting in a photo. Usually her food had gone cold by the time she'd finished taking endless pictures, and so had his, because he didn't like to start his meal unless whoever he was with had started theirs. It was a manners thing.

He liked it that Sophie had no such high pretensions and was simply sitting next to him, clutching her bag of chips, with salt and grease all over her fingers.

'So, Theo, tell me—why did you join the army? Had you always wanted to?'

He thought about how best to answer. 'My father was in the army. He loved it. Sometimes I think he loved the army more than he loved us. I don't remember seeing him very often, but I do remember that when he did come back I had this feeling of…joy and wonder. Here was this man in uniform, fatigues, whatever…a *real* soldier—and he was my dad! I so wanted to be like him. I think… I think I thought it would help me understand him more if I became a soldier, too. That somehow he would know and it would bring him back to me.'

'Back to you? Is your father not around, then?'

He shook his head and scrunched up his empty bag. 'No. My father loved the adventure of travelling the world. We were just a port in a storm. One of many, it turned out.' He heard the bitterness in his voice.

Sophie frowned. 'I don't understand.'

'My father had not just a woman in every port, but *families*. Lots of affairs…lots of illegitimate children. It devastated my mother and she divorced him as soon as she realised. Then she got sick, so I very quickly became the man of the house, looking after my mum and my younger sisters. I really missed him coming home. I really missed having a dad. Once my sisters had flown the nest and I had no responsibilities, I joined the army in the hope that it would bring him back to me.'

'And did it?'

'No.' He smiled ruefully. 'As far as I know

he's living with his latest girlfriend in Buenos Aires.'

'Don't you feel like turning up at his door and confronting him?'

He shook his head. No. 'Why would I chase after someone who doesn't want me?'

That must have struck a chord, because Sophie went silent. Thoughtful. And that was when he remembered that the baby's father—Connor—had not wanted Sophie or their child.

'It's a hard thing to accept,' she said. 'You give your all to someone and sometimes it's just not enough. Not what *they* want. It's like my mother. Whatever I did was never good enough to catch her attention. Never good enough to be important. You can't make someone love you, I guess.'

She scrunched up her own paper bag, all finished.

'No.'

He drove her home, taking her hand to help her out of the car and walking her up the path towards her house to make sure she got in safely.

'Well, I've had a lovely night, Theo. Thank you.'

He nodded and smiled. 'I have, too. It was fun. You've got a great bunch of friends, there.'

'Paramedics can be a better family than your real one sometimes.'

'The army's the same. I've got some good friends I'll have for a lifetime.'

She smiled. 'Well, thank you for bringing me home.'

'My pleasure. It's what friends do.' He smiled.

She reached into her bag for her keys. Paused. Turned and faced him. 'Do you want a coffee before you go?'

He thought about leaving. How he'd feel on the drive home.

Talking about his father always made him feel alone. And what she'd said about her mother had intrigued him. It sounded as if they'd both had a parent who was distracted by other, more interesting things.

It would be good to spend a few more minutes in Sophie's company. Chat to her... He liked her a lot. 'That'd be great—if you're not too tired?'

'I'm good. Come on in.'

He followed her into her home. It was warm and inviting, with some lovely bits of art on the walls—abstract pieces, awash with colour and vigour. He could imagine the artist just throwing paint at the canvas and then smudging a brush through it in insane strokes.

A black cat was curled up on a chair, and it

opened one lazy green eye to assess him briefly before becoming bored.

'That's Magellan. He's the boss of this house. God knows how he'll react when I bring a screaming baby home. He likes his peace and quiet.'

Sophie stroked his head and he began to purr. She kicked off her shoes, groaning at the pleasure of being barefoot, and padded into the kitchen.

He followed her.

Sophie tossed her bag onto the table and grabbed a couple of mugs from the kitchen cupboard. 'Normal or decaf?'

'Whatever you're making.'

She smiled. 'Decaf it is. Take a seat.' She pointed at the kitchen table.

He sat and watched her move around her kitchen with ease. His gaze dropped to her belly. She clearly didn't have long left. Somehow, the dress she was wearing made her look a little bigger than she did when she wore her uniform. He figured it was because it was loose and flowing, but the sight of her blooming and glowing, filled with new life, made him smile.

'What's so funny?' she asked.

'Nothing. So, you're looking very…pregnant. You mentioned Magellan might not be ready for the baby. Are you, do you think?'

She let out a long breath. 'I think so. As much as I can be. I've got all the equipment in. Nappies, clothes, baby wipes, car seat, pram... Oh, and a cot upstairs that I've got to construct—which'll be fun, because I'm useless at following instructions. It'll probably look like a piece of torture equipment by the time I'm done with it.'

'Want me to take a look?'

'Oh, I couldn't ask you to do that!'

'It's no bother. I'm good with my hands.'

Did she blush at that? He thought she did.

He smiled. 'Good at making things,' he clarified. 'I could deconstruct a gun in less than ten seconds.'

She considered him, her head tilted to one side. 'What about putting it together again? Any spare parts left over?'

He laughed. 'Thankfully not. And it always worked again, too.'

'All right,' she said, passing him his mug of coffee. 'I'll let you do the cot.'

'Now?'

She shrugged her shoulders. 'If you want.'

'Lead the way.'

She led him upstairs and he kept his gaze on her bare feet, so that he wasn't staring at her bottom—even though he wanted to. He couldn't help it. He knew he was attracted to her. But she was out of bounds. He liked being with her—that was all.

But he hated saying goodbye to her each day, and then, tonight, he'd had one of the best nights he'd had in a long time—including some great fish and chips on the way home. He knew it was the person he'd spent the time with who counted, and there was something special about Sophie. He wanted to help her. Protect her. Care for her.

It was weird. He never usually felt like this. He could feel stirrings within himself that he'd not expected. It was probably because she was reminding him of how he'd felt when his sisters had got pregnant. It had been a very obvious sign that they were with other men now, and he wasn't needed any more. They were starting new lives. Moving on. And, although he'd dreamed of having his own freedom and being without responsibilities, it had been hard to take that step back and not interfere.

He was used to being a carer. Didn't like the letting go part. He couldn't help it. But sometimes he needed to remind himself that he didn't need to take on anyone else's issues—and Sophie had *plenty*.

But she was a beautiful woman. There would have been something wrong with him if he hadn't noticed. And her being pregnant wasn't putting him off the way it might have at the beginning, before he'd got to know her. The fact that he'd spent a week or more with her now made him feel as if he knew her quite well, and every day he liked her more and more.

Sophie led him into a small room. It was painted white. There was a rocking chair with a foot-rest in one corner, filled with stuffed animals in pale colours. There was a changing unit, piled high with folded baby clothes, and against the wall a large cardboard box—no doubt filled with the pieces of the cot.

'Is that it?'

She nodded, leaning in the doorway. 'You sure you want to do this now?'

'No time like the present. You could go into labour at any moment.'

'Are you saying I'm huge, Theo Finch?' She said it with an amused tone.

He smiled at her and raised his mug of coffee as if in salute. 'Hugely unprepared. What if you had the baby and came home with no cot to put her in? Would you leave her in her car seat whilst you tried to put it together?'

'I'd find a way of making it work.'

'I'm sure… But this is easier—and besides, all that's waiting for me at home is my bed and the prospect of a day off tomorrow, so I can have a late night.'

He turned to open the box and missed the look on Sophie's face that spoke of her tumultuous thoughts.

'Thank you. Shall I leave you to it?' she said.

He turned to face her. 'You can talk to me, if you'd like. Here, let me move all those cuddly toys and you can put your feet up.'

He scooped up all the plushies in one go and set them down on the floor, away from where he'd be working. Sophie settled into the rocker with a sigh, resting her hands on her swollen abdomen.

Theo got busy pulling out all the pieces, locating the instructions and checking that he had all the screws, nuts and bolts needed for the project. The pack helpfully included an Allen key.

'Seems straightforward enough. If only life came with instructions...'

She laughed. 'We'd all screw up less.'

He gathered the first two pieces for assembly. 'When did you screw up?'

'When I chose the father of my baby.'

'Were you trying to get pregnant with Connor?'

Sophie shook her head. 'It was an accident.'

'Then you didn't know that he was a bad choice. You picked him as a partner—not a potential parent.'

'But I *thought* he'd be a good parent. How wrong could I be? Ouch! She's kicking me. Probably telling me off for bad-mouthing her father.'

'Can I?' He indicated that he'd like to touch her belly to feel the baby.

She blushed a delightful rose colour. 'Sure.'

He smiled back as she took his hand and guided it over her bump to where the kicks were. He concentrated, waiting to feel something, and then—*bam!* A little kick. Right in the centre of the palm of his hand.

'Wow! She's strong.'

Sophie agreed. 'She is, isn't she?'

When he became aware that maybe her hand upon his and his hand upon her belly was perhaps a little more intimate than he'd been expecting, he pulled his hand free to continue building the cot. He was glad to be able to look away from her, because his cheeks were flaming hot.

What was the matter with him? He'd hardly been drinking—he'd been on orange juice all night! Or did vitamin C make your head woozy? He'd have to check on that later.

But for now he carried on, screwing into place all the slats to go under the mattress. That was the longest part of the process. After that it could only have been maybe thirty minutes or so before Sophie had a completed cot.

'What do you think?' he asked with pride.

'It's amazing! Thank you.' She held out her hand and he helped her up into a standing position.

'Tell me whereabouts you want it.'

'Over in that corner, please.' She pointed.

He hefted the sturdy cot over to the corner and then picked up all the toys he'd moved earlier and put them inside.

'How does it feel to know that a baby will be sleeping in here soon?'

Sophie suddenly looked so uncertain, so apprehensive.

'What's wrong? What did I say?'

She seemed to think for a moment, as if deciding whether to share her innermost thoughts with him. Then, 'What if I do it all wrong?'

'What makes you think that'll happen?'

'My mother was never the greatest role model for being a mum. What if I'm like her? Distant? Not interested in my child? I want to continue to do my job. What if my child feels pushed away, the way I felt with my mother?'

He didn't really think. He just went straight over to her and pulled her into his arms for a hug. 'Hey, it'll be fine.'

'I know. I just…'

For the moment they continued to hug. Theo could understand her fears. If all she'd known was a mother who didn't seem to notice her, then of course she might feel she'd turn out the same way. But sometimes having a bad parent showed you how you *didn't* want to be. Made you determined to walk an alternative path and do things differently. *Better.*

He squeezed her tight, loving the way she felt against him, all soft and her hair scented with shampoo. It felt good to hold her. To make her feel better. To assuage her fears and worries.

What would it be like if this were *his* baby in her belly? If this was *their* home and he was the one waiting for this baby to be born so that he could hold it too?

The feelings he felt were so terrifying he almost pushed her away, but he knew he couldn't do that. He would never be so cruel. And besides, this wasn't about him. It wasn't his baby. He had nothing to worry about. So why was he holding her? Comforting her?

I shouldn't be doing this.

Sophie must have felt the change in him, and she lifted her head to look at him, as if to check that he was okay.

Theo looked down into her eyes. Such a deep blue. Like a clear Caribbean sea. She held such wonder in those eyes of hers. Such concern.

Such hope. Such…desire? He looked at her mouth, at her lips parting as she breathed.

Would it be wrong to take advantage of this moment? Should he be a gentleman and walk away?

'Sophie, we shouldn't do this…'

He saw her glance at his mouth, and he wanted to kiss her so much it almost tore him in two! But she wasn't his. Wasn't meant to be his. And this wasn't how friends should be with each other.

So why was his body telling him to throw caution to the wind and friendship be damned? Telling him that kissing her would be the most wonderful thing in this world?

'No, we shouldn't…'

But her words didn't match her actions. He could see it in her glazed eyes, her dilated pupils, that she wanted him to kiss her, and the temptation to do so was so strong he wasn't sure if he was strong enough to walk away.

Then he felt her daughter kick him again, and it was like a bucket of cold water thrown over him.

He *couldn't* kiss her. This wasn't just about her! There was a baby involved. A little baby girl who would need her father. And he wasn't that. And he couldn't make Sophie's life any more complicated than it already was.

If he was her friend, as he kept insisting that he was, he needed to walk away. To hell with this attraction. This need. This want.

With sadness and deep regret, he took a step back.

'I'm sorry, Soph.'

CHAPTER FIVE

SOPHIE WAS IN a state of disbelief. She had been in his arms, pressed against him, enjoying the feel of him, the warmth, the sense of safety she'd felt. He'd asked her about how she felt about becoming a mother, and just for a brief moment she had felt absolute terror. Had shared with him her innermost fears, practically blurting them out, needing to say them. Get them out in the open.

At work, in front of other people, she managed to maintain a calm façade—she was a woman who could roll with the punches. She was strong...she could cope. It didn't matter that Connor had deserted them.

But at home, alone, she often worried over her doubts. Especially late at night and as the time for her to give birth became imminent. It could happen tonight, tomorrow, the next day... and then her entire life would be different.

She wanted to be the best mum she could be

to her daughter—but what if she wasn't? What if she was like her mother? She'd left as soon as she could. Bolted the second she'd thought Sophie was old enough to look after herself, not realising that Sophie had been doing that already for years.

Even when her mother had been around Sophie had been a dutifully quiet child, knowing that she would never get the attention from her mother that she craved. She had learned to take care of herself at an early age and her expectations of her mother had been low.

How would she make sure she could meet her child's needs? Or even her own, when she had a child and a career to take care of? In that moment when Theo had asked her it had all seemed too much. And for him to hold her like that had been everything. He would never fully know or understand just how much she had needed to be held in that moment. To be taken care of by someone else.

And then he'd nearly kissed her.

She'd wanted it. Oh, how she had wanted it! To feel him press his lips against hers... To give in to her desires and to hell with the consequences...

But Theo had been the stronger of the two of them.

Perhaps that was a good thing? Someone had needed to be sensible there.

No. Let's face it, he was probably trying to save me any embarrassment. He wouldn't be interested in someone like me. I clearly come with a whole truckload of baggage.

She stepped away from him now, reluctantly letting go, but nodding frantically. 'No, of course not. It was just a silly moment. It's late...we're both tired...it's been a long day.'

He stared at her then, and she hated his scrutiny.

'I ought to go. Leave you to it,' he said.

She nodded. 'Yes. Thank you for doing the baby's cot. I really appreciate that.'

'It was no problem.'

She pushed past him and headed down the stairs, hearing his footsteps behind her. Her cheeks were flushed with a raging heat, and when she got to the bottom she opened the front door wide, glad of the cool air that blew in.

'Well, goodnight, Theo.'

'Night, Soph.'

Another brisk nod. 'Drive safe.'

He passed her, stood on the front path and looked back. 'I will. Take care.'

'You too.'

And she closed the door, sinking back against it, registering what a huge mistake the pair of them had just evaded. Theo might be hot, and he might be the kind of guy that filled her dreams, but in real life Theo wanted no more commitment from her than Connor did.

He'd told her enough times that he was there to be her friend, but even that, she believed at heart, was in doubt. Men like him didn't stick around for women like her. Especially now she'd revealed her deepest, darkest fears. He must think she was going to be a right flop as a parent. It was pathetic, really.

How could I have been so stupid?

No. They'd both had a lucky escape. There was no point in falling for her hunky student, no matter how good-looking he was and how erotic her dreams about him might be.

She had no time or place for men who only wanted fun.

She was about to become a mother.

Good mothers put their children first, and that meant not having casual guys hanging around, dipping in and out of her bed.

She needed to put some distance between herself and Theo, so as not to be tempted again.

Sophie had had a bad night's sleep. She'd tossed and turned constantly, unable to get into a comfy position, as her mind had helpfully replayed that moment in her baby's nursery.

What the hell would have happened if they'd kissed?

Well, apart from feeling amazing at the time, I think afterwards would have been pretty embarrassing!

Would it have stopped at a kiss? Would she have wanted more? Would he?

They both knew where they stood. She wasn't looking for a new man and Theo most definitely wasn't father material. He was a fun-loving guy who wasn't looking to settle down and who didn't do commitment, which she'd thought made him safe to be around.

But maybe they ought to have adult supervision now, after spending the night laughing together and dancing? An old-fashioned chaperone? Because she had to face it: she wasn't just dealing with normal physical attraction here. These damned pregnancy hormones had a part to play, too. It was as if she wasn't really herself, but had been taken over by an inner demon that wanted and yearned and desired.

There was a spark between them. It was undeniable. She knew he'd felt it, too, before common sense had kicked in—and thank God it had!

She smiled now, as she put her breakfast things into the dishwasher. They were okay. Neither of them had done anything they shouldn't, and they would carry on as normal when they met again.

All she had to do today was grab her swimsuit and a towel and get ready for her pregnancy aqua fitness class. She went every weekend and had been going since she was about six months pregnant.

It felt good to be in the water. It supported her body—especially her heavy belly—and she always felt wonderful afterwards. Plus, it was a bonding experience. She was getting to know some other mothers-to-be, and one or two of them were going to be single parents, like her. She'd talked to them after class, found out how they were going to cope. But each of them seemed to have someone to call on. Someone to be a birth partner. Someone to help in those first few difficult weeks.

It made her feel less alone to have these new friends, but at the same time it made her see how isolated she really was. A lifetime of being independent and looking after herself had somehow kept people at a polite distance. She had her paramedics family, but she needed to have a postnatal family, too—because when this baby came she wouldn't be able to hang out at the ambulance station or meet her colleagues when they dropped their patients off at the hospitals. They'd be gone. Working. Theo would be back at university.

She'd have to start letting people in. Trusting them.

But how did you do that?

How did she put trust in other people when all she'd ever done was only trust herself?

Theo found himself clock-watching. He'd last seen Sophie just over eleven hours ago and already he missed her. He found that to be something that disturbed him greatly.

She was someone he considered just a friend. He didn't want to get attached to this beautiful woman. She was about to become a mother. Her whole world would shift and change, her priorities would become different, and he could not expect that a relationship with her would be successful because he wasn't looking for the type of commitment that Sophie and her daughter, would need. Plus, there was all her history with the baby's father, and from what he had heard none of that was really settled...

But he couldn't stop thinking about her.

Why was that?

He thought about how he'd felt each time his sisters had been pregnant. He'd worried about them. Had asked them to phone him the second they went into labour so he could be there. It had seemed the natural thing to do. He'd been like a father to his siblings after their actual father had deserted them. He'd been their carer. Their protector. He'd nursed his mother through her last days, trying to hide as much of it as he could from his sisters, and the burden he'd been under had been immense.

All that fear, all that pain, all that grief...he'd kept it all under wraps to protect his sisters, leaving almost no time to take care of himself because he had Leonora, Hazel and Martha to worry about.

And yet there was this unwanted physical desire for Sophie. Something that pulled at him. Which, again, blew his mind—because, if he'd been told a few months ago that he would want to kiss or fall into bed with a heavily pregnant woman he would have looked incredulous and laughed his head off. That was not the type of woman he looked for when he wanted to share some adult fun on occasion.

Perhaps it would be best if he maintained some sort of professional distance?

No. I made that stupid bet with her that she could depend on me for at least a year...and I don't break my promises. I'm not my dad.

He couldn't walk away—not now. Not like Connor had. Not like her mother had. Not like his own father had.

He knew how painful it was to be the one left behind. How it made you feel. Unworthy. Unloved. Unimportant. As if you weren't good enough to stick around for.

Maybe once his placement with her was over he would start to distance himself? For his own protection. He didn't need to go making any stupid mistakes with a mother-to-be! Imagine how complicated *that* would be! No, he would finish his placement, keep in touch on occasion, as promised, and maybe just send Christmas cards or something? Back away slowly. Not get too involved. Do what he did best when things got complicated with women.

So why did having these particular thoughts make him feel so bad? It wasn't as if he was walking away from the mother of *his* child. Her baby was nothing to do with him! She'd been in that situation before he'd even arrived on the scene.

Maybe he felt so rubbish because he'd promised to be reliable, someone she could trust, and already he was thinking of his exit strategy?

I'll just play it day by day. Besides, she might be the one to get rid of me!

They might have a huge falling out—who knew how she felt this morning, after last night's near miss? She was probably already regretting it. She might even be the one to let *him* off the hook! To tell him to forget the bet, that it didn't matter any more, that all bets were off and he could go back to his normal life.

And then he would be able to walk away without feeling any guilt. Start again. Find someone single—someone who wasn't already writing a birth plan would be good.

He sighed, knowing that wouldn't make it better either, and then did what he always did when he got confused. He called his little sister Martha.

'Hey, it's me.'

'Hey, you. How's it going?'

He smiled at the usual greeting. 'Fine.'

'Oh-oh. I don't like the sound of that. Come on, spill—who is she?'

Theo sighed. 'Sophie.'

'Sophie? As in *paramedic* Sophie? The one you're doing your training with?'

'That's the one.'

He waited for the barrage of abuse.

'Are you stupid? Wait! Didn't you say she's hugely pregnant?'

'Yeah.'

'Wow, Theo! It doesn't take you long, does it?'

He smiled.

'You haven't…um…you know…done the deed?'

'Of course not! She's pregnant.'

'So? A woman doesn't stop being a sexual being just because she's about to drop a sprog.'

'You have such a poetic way with words, Marth. Remind me again what you do for a living?' Martha was an English teacher, with aspirations to write a book. 'Nothing happened. We just…nearly kissed.'

'How do you "nearly" kiss someone?'

'We were going to. I backed off at the last minute. It's too complicated.'

'It certainly is. I would have thought she'd be the last type of woman you'd get the hots for.'

'Yeah, me too.'

'I'm sure everything's fine. You didn't do it. You thought with your head, rather than that other thing you guys have got going on, and for that I'm proud of you.'

'Thanks. I think…'

Martha was silent for a minute and he could tell she was mulling something over.

'What?' he asked.

'Have you ever thought that…?' She sighed. 'I don't know… That maybe one day you would *want* to settle down? With a family? You did a great job with us, and sometimes you just seem so…'

'What?'

'Lonely.'

He said nothing. It wasn't a thought he wanted to entertain.

'Look, I've got to go. Leo is waking up and he'll want a nappy-change.'

'All right.'

'You make an excellent father-figure, Theo. To other people's kids. I'm just saying it in case you need to hear it.'

Theo smiled. He wasn't meant to have a favourite sister, but Martha definitely came close.

'I love you, Martha.'

'I love you, too.'

CHAPTER SIX

SOPHIE WAS FEELING apprehensive on Monday morning. She'd had a whole weekend free of Theo, wondering how he might be with her when they met again. Not that they'd actually done anything. No one had stepped over a line, no rules had been broken, but… But she had stared deeply into his eyes, hoping, clearly *asking* for his kiss, and she'd not been able to stop wondering how far it would have gone if Theo *had* kissed her…

She knew he was a guy who wanted nothing more from a woman than to have a bit of fun on a temporary basis, so technically she'd had a lucky break. It was good that he'd stopped it when he had, because they might have slept together, and then he would have expected everything to be normal.

She didn't need the complications of dealing with the aftermath—the awkwardness, the not being able to meet each other's eyes, the knowledge that once he'd got the grand prize he didn't want to be with her any more.

He'd made it quite clear that he wasn't the settling down type and yet… She couldn't help but wonder. Theo had the look of a guy who would be good in bed and good with kids. And being pregnant, being flooded with hormones that made her want and need, that was an explosive cocktail.

When he'd held her close she'd felt the heat of his body, the solidity of it, his hardness against her softness. She'd smelled the scent of him. Felt security within his arms. His gaze had matched hers when her lips had parted, almost tempted…

It's a good thing that nothing happened.

At his usual time she saw him arrive, and he gave her a huge smile as he approached.

Sophie let out a sigh of relief.

Good, it wouldn't be awkward. Thank God for that!

'Morning. You ready for another full-on week?' she asked.

'Yep! Are you?'

'Always.'

They both checked the vehicle, adding some extra supplies they might need, and then called in to Control that they were ready for calls.

One came in almost immediately.

'Six zero two, we've got a category one call. Male, age unknown, breathing difficulties, found collapsed in the street.'

Control gave them the approximate address and they hit the lights and the sirens.

'What do you think it is?' Theo asked.

Her mind conjured up many things. 'Breathing difficulties could mean anything. Joe Public can't always accurately describe what he's witnessing, so it could be someone having an asthma attack, it could be cardiac-related, or respiratory, or something else entirely. He could be drunk and passed out.'

She concentrated on driving them safely through the traffic. If someone was having breathing difficulties seconds could be vital in saving a life, and she needed to make sure her focus was on the road, on the other drivers, bikers, and even on pedestrians, who were sometimes known to absently step into the road, seemingly without hearing the siren or seeing the lights blazing and coming towards them. Mobile phones had a lot to answer for...

They pulled up next to a crowd of people, gathered around a man in his mid to late twenties who was slumped up against a shop window. He didn't look good. He'd obviously been sick, and the onlookers had a mix of disgusted, pale expressions as they gawped at the scene, intrigued by what was must be an interesting event on their way to work.

'I've been trying to move him so I can do CPR,' said a young man wearing a grey suit, holding his hands out in front of him, covered in the man's excretions.

Sophie put gloves on and knelt down to lay two fingers against the patient's neck to check for a pulse. 'Has he been able to communicate with you? Do you know his name?'

'No, I just found him like that. He's cold and…stiff.'

Sophie looked up at Theo and shook her head. They were too late. By the look of this patient—his clothes, the marks on his arms—this young man had succumbed to the misuse of drugs. It was a very sad scene.

'Could you get one of the blankets from the car, Theo? And can you get—sorry, what's your name?'

'Jack.'

'Can you get Jack something to clean himself up with?'

Theo got various things from the car, passing paper towels and antibacterial gel to Jack before he covered the patient with a blanket and stood by whilst Sophie she called in to Control, asking them to notify the police that they were with a dead body.

'Already en route, six zero two.'

'Thanks, Control.'

'Are you okay?' Control asked.

'We're good.'

'And your student?'

She looked at Theo. He seemed all right. This wasn't any way for anyone to start their week, but Theo was no green student still in his teens. He was a fully-grown man and he'd been in the army. Surely he'd seen a dead body before? His face looked stern.

'He's okay. But if anything crops up I'll notify you.'

'We'll tell your station, so when you get back he can be assigned someone to talk to if he needs it. And we'll let his university know.'

'That's great. Thank you, Control.'

The ambulance service was very good at looking after their own. A lot of hardened paramedics were used to seeing death, and some even developed a gallows humour to deal with it. But every time they dealt with a death Control would still check on the team involved, to make sure they were okay and give them time off and counselling if they needed it.

Theo was trying to keep the growing crowd back. 'Is there anyone here who recognises him? Saw what happened?' he was asking.

Sophie smiled inwardly. He was doing the

right thing. They needed the crowd to move back because the police would want to examine the area. It was an unexpected death on a public street, so they would want to take statements from the onlookers. Theo was going to make a great paramedic. His instincts were in the right place.

Eventually she began to hear the wail of police sirens, and soon they were surrounded by officers and the crew of the ambulance that would be needed to take the body to the nearest hospital morgue.

Once they'd given their assessment to the police and handed over the case, checking one last time to make sure that Jack was okay, they packed up and got back into the car.

'You all right?' she asked Theo.

'Yeah. I'm good. Are you?'

She nodded. 'Have you seen a dead body before?'

He nodded. 'Unfortunately.'

'Do you want to talk about it?'

He shook his head. 'Just army stuff. I'm all right.'

'You're sure?' He didn't look all right, she thought.

'You see death in the army. Stationed overseas—in Afghanistan...other places with active shooting—you almost expect it, in a way.

Harden yourself to it. You're fighting for a cause. You know you're there to try and do the right thing. You forget that not everyone can cope with that type of stresses.'

She understood. 'Who did you lose?'

His voice softened. 'A good friend. Matt. Matty-Boy, we all called him.'

'What happened?'

'I would have said it was nothing out of the ordinary for us. We were infantry. We'd been in skirmishes, firefights, ambushes. The usual. We dealt with it in our downtime by playing footy, cards, making jokes, riling each other up. We thought we were fine. We kept an eye on each other...made sure we were all okay.'

He paused briefly.

'One night, after a skirmish in which we found an entire family had been killed, Matty-Boy took his own life.'

'Oh, Theo...' She couldn't imagine how he must have felt.

'I didn't see the signs. I thought he was okay. He seemed okay. Until he wasn't.'

'Is that why you left the army?'

He nodded. 'It added to it. The guilt I felt at missing the signs...it ate me up for a while.'

She wanted to lay her hand on his. To show him that she was there. That she cared. That she understood how he was hurting. But she was afraid to. What if it was misinterpreted? It was so soon after last night…

Dammit! He's hurting.

She laid her hand on his, wrapped her fingers around his. Squeezed. 'If you ever want to talk about him I'd love to hear about who he was. What he meant to you. His life…'

'Thanks. I'm okay, though.'

And he pulled his hand out from under hers.

She tried not to feel hurt at the small rejection, but knew her previous assessment of him had been correct. He was strong. That was good. He would need that in this job. He was able to separate his feelings and control them, not let them overwhelm him.

'Let's grab coffees to go. Get some breakfast.'

He smiled. 'Great idea.'

She drove them to a small supermarket where they quickly bought what they needed, and they were on their way back to their vehicle when Control called in with another job. Multiple units, including the fire brigade, were being dispatched to an address where two patients had been found together, collapsed in their front room. One female in her seventies and an male who was eighty.

'Odd…we don't often get two people together

like that,' Sophie said, already trying to imagine in her head what had happened.

The address wasn't far from them, and they managed to get to the property within six minutes of the call coming in.

'Grab the jump bag and the oxygen,' she told Theo.

They'd arrived first, and a young woman in her forties was waiting for them at the door. 'They're in the lounge. They're breathing, but I can't wake them up!'

Sophie rushed in, her eyes scanning for danger. Had there been a break-in? An attack? If so, she had to be mindful that the assailant might still be there, or that a weapon might be around. But nothing looked disturbing except for the fact that there was an elderly couple, each in their respective chairs, completely unconscious, their faces pink.

The gas fire was on, as it had turned a little cooler... Carbon monoxide poisoning? Carbon monoxide was tasteless, had no smell, and it was colourless. If the fireplace was faulty it might have been issuing out poisonous fumes within the room.

As Sophie rushed to check for pulses, she turned to Theo and the woman. 'Open all the doors and windows!'

'What's going on?' asked the young woman.

Was she their daughter?

'It could be carbon monoxide. Can you turn that fire off?'

The woman hurried to do so.

'Theo, I'm going to need you to help me carry these two out of here. We'll do airways and oxygen once we've got them outside. It's too dangerous for us to stay.'

She was thinking about her baby. If it *was* carbon monoxide poisoning—which she strongly suspected—what effect might it have on her growing child?

The pinkness in her patients' faces was a dead giveaway. Carbon monoxide, once breathed in, would enter the bloodstream and mix with a person's haemoglobin in the blood cells that carried oxygen around the body to form carboxyhaemoglobin. When that occurred, the blood wasn't able to carry the oxygen the body needed, therefore causing cell and tissue death.

Theo shook his head. 'No. You two get out now! Go on—I can't have you in here. I'll get them out one by one.'

'But I'm the senior para—'

Theo grabbed her arm. 'You're *pregnant*,' he said. 'Your rank means nothing in this situation. Now, go!'

He was right. But she was fighting against

her training, which drummed into them the fact that you never approached a patient or a scene without checking for your own safety first. She should be the one protecting Theo! Not letting him sacrifice himself for these two patients. He was the student. The observer.

But she'd barely detected a pulse in the man…it might already be too late!

In the end her training was no match for the instinct she felt to protect her unborn child and she hurried out, pulling the other woman with her, only to find that outside a fire engine was arriving, the crew jumping out, dressed and ready for action.

She quickly apprised them of the situation and two firemen rushed in wearing breathing apparatus to help Theo bring out the first patient. The rest of fire crew brought out the second and laid her on the grass next to Theo and Sophie, who applied oxygen masks to their faces and turned them on full.

The elderly couple weren't looking great. Completely unconscious.

An ambulance crew loaded the patients into their vehicle and went screaming off into the distance just as a firefighter came out, removing his mask.

'We've switched the gas off at the mains. Looks like there was a blocked flue in the chimney. You've both been exposed to the gas, so you really ought to go and get yourselves checked out.'

'Okay.' Sophie nodded and looked at Theo. 'You okay?'

'I feel fine—it's just not the start to Monday morning that I'd expected.'

Neither had she. After such a great Friday night spent with Theo, and a wonderful relaxing weekend, she'd expected the usual high-octane week of racing from call to call, but to get a death straight away and then this...

And now they would have to go to hospital to get themselves checked out. That would take her and her vehicle off the road, and they couldn't afford to be a crew down. And what about Theo's training? He'd lose a whole day.

She'd been exposed for...what?...a minute? Was that enough to harm her? Or her child? She couldn't take that risk. That was what was most important here.

At the hospital, a doctor checked them over.

'Could it harm my baby?' asked Sophie. 'I wasn't in the property for long.'

The doctor nodded in understanding. 'We'll check your bloods, but for now I want you both to have some oxygen therapy.' He attached masks to their faces and turned on the flow. 'I'm sure your baby will be fine. It's long-term exposure to carbon monoxide that we worry about, and you say you were only in the room for less than a minute? Let's keep you on the oxygen for a short while, and then we'll carry out an ultrasound, just to be on the safe side.'

Sophie nodded. 'Do you know how the couple are?'

The doctor shrugged. 'They're still alive. They appear to have been exposed the night before, plus they're both smokers, so the levels in their blood will be high. We might have to try hyperbaric therapy if they're to survive this.'

An oxygen chamber...

'How long do we have to wear the oxygen masks?' Sophie asked.

'Not long. I'll just check the carboxyhaemoglobin levels and if they're really low, or non-existent, then you can go.'

'Thank you, Doctor.'

He nodded and left.

Sophie looked at Theo, appreciative of how he'd thought to protect her and her baby. 'You were great back there, you know?'

'I was just doing my job.'

'You were putting the patients first.'

'So were you. I had to order you out of there.'

She nodded. He had. He'd stepped right up, knowing he was the stronger one of the two of them—the one who could risk remaining in the room a little longer than her. She appreciated what he had done for her and her baby. He had proved again that he could be relied upon.

Sometimes being a first responder you forgot that you were always the one running *towards* danger, when everyone else was running *from* it. But Control was very good about her current situation, and only sent her to jobs where she could play the part of rapid response paramedic. She knew she would always have backup. Knew that others would be right behind her.

It was easy to forget how dangerous life could be—and she had a precious little one on board whom she needed to think about, too. Maybe she should slow down? Consider exactly what she should be doing now? Change her mindset from thinking just about herself to becoming a *mum*. A job that came with a whole new set of dangers and risks and worries...

'I don't leave people behind,' he said.

Of course. Army guy. He would have been committed to his fellow soldiers. They would have had a code. They would have been honourable. They'd have looked out for one another.

Theo, even though he was the trainee, the subordinate, had been the one to order her out of the house to keep her and her baby safe. To stop her from inhaling any more of the carbon monoxide than she had already. He'd put her first. Her baby first. She could never thank him enough for that.

He was going to make a fantastic paramedic. Whomever he got paired with would totally be able to rely on him, she had no doubt. She'd worked alone for so long, she'd almost forgotten that she didn't need to be the one in charge all the time—that on occasion she could rely on and trust someone else to look out for her.

She wasn't a lone ranger. She had Theo and Control and the whole ambulance service watching her back.

In that moment, looking at him as he sat with an oxygen mask clamped to his face, she felt her feelings for him grow. She could actually feel them. Could feel gratitude and appreciation and love for what he had done swell within her.

He was a good man. A kind man.

She thought of him out in Afghanistan, fighting, finding his friend Matty-Boy dead, all the things he must have seen, the things he must have gone through. Experienced.

He was brave.

He was a man she felt she could trust professionally, and that was what you needed when you worked in a team as paramedics. You had to know that you could rely on your partner, and Sophie knew that she could rely on Theo.

But personally…? On a romantic level…?

She knew she wanted him to be right for her, but she also knew that they didn't stand a chance. They might both have been abandoned by a parent, but they wanted different things because of it. He was in her life but he was a mayfly—a beautiful thing that would only last for a short time. She should appreciate him whilst he was with her.

'You know…we've never really had a chance to speak about what nearly happened the other night,' she said.

He turned to look at her, his hand clutching his oxygen mask.

'I know I really wanted to kiss you, and I think you really wanted to kiss me,' she went on. 'At least, I hope you did. I hope I'm not so unattractive like this that you would recoil.' She laughed, feeling almost embarrassed.

'You're beautiful, Soph. Pregnant or otherwise. Don't let anyone tell you anything different.'

She smiled behind the oxygen mask. He made her feel glad.

'And, for the record, I wanted to kiss you very much.'

She nodded, staring at her hero in the other bed and feeling glad that he was by her side as a partner, even if it was just at work.

She knew that if she were to keep him in her life he'd need to understand that she wasn't going to be like those women in his past who'd got clingy. She was nothing like that—even if she did find herself wondering what it might be like to be with him.

But that was just stuff and nonsense—hormones and her baby brain, looking for dreams and perfection and happily-ever-afters when she knew that she could never have that with Theo.

She would just have to bask in his presence temporarily. Enjoy the brief time she would share with him before he moved on and became someone else's hero.

She would cope with his loss.

She'd dealt with loss her entire life.

It had become an old friend.

Theo breathed in his oxygen. So they'd almost kissed? So what? It didn't mean anything. It had been a brief weakness. They'd both gone a little too far after an evening of fun together, creating the illusion of something else that wasn't truly there. It had brought them close, and then he had built her baby's cot, comforted her when she'd got scared. It had been a moment, that was all.

So why did he feel that he was somehow letting her down? And not just *her*, but also himself? Was it because she was pregnant? Was it because he felt as if he'd messed with a woman he really ought not to have? She was going to be a mother! She had a life and a history with someone else—this Connor, the father of her baby.

Even if he wasn't around, he was still there, lurking in the recesses of her mind. She might think things were over for her and Connor, but what if that all changed when the baby arrived? People did that. Didn't realise what they'd lost until it actually became a reality. What if this Connor had simply failed to connect with the fact that Sophie saying *'I'm pregnant'* meant that there was going to be a real baby he would have to deal with one day? Once his daughter was born, he might feel differently. Who knew?

And when this other man eventually came crawling out from under the rock where he'd been living for the last few months, finally having admitted his mistake, did Theo really want to have developed *feelings* for this woman? Feelings he would then have to deny?

Absolutely not!

Theo didn't need *complicated*. He didn't need the problems that getting involved with a woman who was having a baby by someone else would bring.

She was going to have a baby. A brand-new baby girl who hadn't been let down by the world yet. She was completely innocent, and she deserved to have the best start in life possible when she was born, to be brought into the world by people who loved her.

Sophie might think things were over with Connor, but Theo knew differently.

His sister Hazel had split with her partner once. She had told everyone that it was all over between her and David, that he was an idiot, and a child, and she would have nothing to do with him ever again. But they had a son together, and when that boy had been admitted to hospital with suspected meningitis—thankfully it hadn't been—it had brought Hazel and David back together again and they were a family now. Happy and content.

Theo didn't want to get in the way of something that might not yet be over. But still... despite his rules about not getting involved... he was finding it really hard to tell himself that he needed not to think of Sophie in *that way.*

It was difficult, because he'd really enjoyed that night they'd spent at Ross's party, and he knew her quite well now, and he liked everything he saw. She was intelligent, dedicated, funny. She made him laugh and smile and he looked forward to every shift he had with her—didn't like having to say goodbye each evening.

He kept finding his thoughts running to her. What was she doing? Where was she? Was she all right? Was she happy? It was important to him that she be happy. And, weirdly, he found that he felt an intense, irrational anger towards this Connor for having hurt her. For having royally screwed up an opportunity to be with this wonderful woman who was having *his baby*, for crying out loud! Was the man *stupid*?

When the doctor came back and told them that the carboxyhaemoglobin levels in their blood were barely traceable, and they could go, with relief, the pair of them removed their oxygen masks and thanked the staff for taking care of them.

'Next time you come here just bring us *other* patients. Don't be the patients yourselves, you hear?' the doctor said with a smile.

They promised they would do their best.

'We've got a trauma call for you. Fifty-two-year-old male, fallen from a ladder, suspected broken arms.'

Arms. Plural. Ouch!

Sophie drove to the address and could see their patient lying on the paved driveway by a ladder. A woman, probably the patient's wife, came scurrying up to their vehicle as they got out.

'He fell off the ladder taking down the Christmas lights. I told him to get them down months ago, but he wouldn't listen.'

Sophie pulled on gloves as she walked towards the patient, Theo following behind with the jump bag and Entonox.

'You don't look like you've got long to go,' said the woman.

'I'm imminent.'

'You should be at home, putting your feet up.'

Sophie smiled. She got that a lot. But she'd go stir crazy at home. Working was much better—even if it did tire her out. All her scans and blood tests and BP checks told her that she was doing fine, and it wasn't as if she was ill. She could still do her job.

'What's your husband's name?' she asked.

'Jeff.'

'Any medical issues we need to know about?'

'Does lazy-itis count?'

Sophie smiled as she knelt down so that Jeff could see her. He was face-down, but she could see a bad graze across his cheek.

'Hello, Jeff. I'm Sophie, and I've got my colleague Theo here, too. Can you tell me what happened?'

'I was taking down the damned lights and the ladder must have slipped.'

'You put your arms out to break your fall?'

'Yeah. Felt something go…heard something crack.'

'What hurts the most?'

'My arms. My right knee.'

'Okay…and if you could rate your pain from zero to ten, with zero being no pain and ten being the worst…?'

'Definitely a nine.'

Sophie looked to Theo and mouthed *Entonox*.

Theo got the canister and the mouthpiece ready. Ideally, they liked the patient to hold the mouthpiece, but on this occasion the patient's arms were out of commission, so Theo kept hold of the mouthpiece so that Jeff could breathe from it.

'Nice deep breaths, mate,' Theo said. 'You can breathe out as well as in…breathe through it.'

They were going to need help, log-rolling this patient. Because of the fall he might have a neck or spinal injury, and with Theo controlling the Entonox, and Sophie pregnant, they would need extra hands—and soon.

She radioed through to Control and asked them what the running time was on the second crew with an ambulance.

'En route, six zero two. ETA two minutes.'

'Thanks.' She knelt down again to explain the situation to Jeff. 'I'm going to give you a painkilling injection. It will help until they get here, okay? All you need to do is breathe, try to relax, and don't move anything.'

After giving him the injection, she tried to check out the rest of his body. They'd need to get a cervical collar on him, but that would be impossible until the extra help arrived. His arms were most definitely broken, and she thought he'd either broken his kneecap or maybe even his lower leg near the knee joint from his impact with the paving slabs from such a height.

When the ambulance crew arrived she smiled to see her friends Ross and Cameron. In a co-ordinated effort they managed to log-roll their patient and get the collar on, plus two arm splints and one on Jeff's right leg. Then Ross and Cameron loaded Jeff into their vehicle.

'You look after yourself, Jeff, all right?' she told him.

Jeff smiled, despite the pain he was in. 'Will do. Looks like those lights will have to stay up all year, huh? You can tell the missus I won't be going up any ladders any time soon.'

Sophie smiled in return. 'It's not that long till Christmas again, anyway.'

Theo closed the ambulance doors and then they both cleared up their equipment and got everything loaded back into the vehicle. There was about an hour left of their shift, and without any calls coming in Theo asked her about their previous patients.

'Do we ever get to find out how they're doing?'

'Occasionally. If we end up at the same hospital we can always ask.'

'I thought I'd be fine, not knowing how the story ends, but as it turns out I'm curious.'

Sophie glanced at him and smiled. 'It happens—but you can console yourself with the fact that you got there first, you treated someone and got them the help they need. You began their story. Everything after that is out of your hands. You have to learn to let go.'

He nodded, but she could see he was clearly thinking about something.

'Did you choose to be a paramedic because you thought you wouldn't have to get involved?' she asked him.

He shrugged. 'Maybe a little. I thought I could care for people a little bit and then just let them go on their merry way to hospital, my part done.'

'Is that what you're used to? Only having a bit-part in people's lives?'

He was silent. Clearly the question made him uncomfortable.

'If it makes you feel any better, that's what I'm used to. This works for me,' she said.

'But you reached out once. Tried to be more than a bit-part in Connor's life.'

'I thought he was *"the one"*.' She shrugged. 'Turned out I was wrong.'

'If only people came with bright neon signs flashing above their heads—that would make it easier, don't you think?' he asked.

She looked at him, considering. 'Don't you ever find yourself wondering what if…? I mean, what if you've already walked away from the woman who could have been the absolute love of your life?'

Theo laughed. 'I'm hoping that I'd be clever enough to recognise her.'

'And if you did? Would you finally settle down, do you think?'

He seemed to think about her words. 'I don't know.'

'Not even for true love?'

Theo went quiet again. Clearly, she'd made him think.

What was he so scared of? Was it just of commitment to one person? Was he one of those guys who was so in love with the idea of playing the field that he couldn't bear the idea of settling for just one woman? She hoped not. She hoped he was more than that. Because it seemed like he cared so much! His heart was in the right place with his family, and with his patients, but what about when it came to his own heart? Was he afraid to give it to someone?

'I just find it hard to understand,' she said. 'All my life I've wanted love. Craved it, even. I was so independent as a child. Dutiful, never getting into trouble, never wanting to bother my parents with having to pay attention to me. It was like I kind of knew they weren't capable of it, you know…? So when I grew up I was ready for love. I'd been starved of it for years. Maybe that was my mistake? Seeing it in Connor because I wanted to. I wanted to see something that wasn't there, when in actual fact I'd fallen for a man who was just as incapable of showing me love as my parents were.'

'Are they both still alive?' Theo asked.

'Mum is. As far as I know. My dad died when I was young.'

He frowned. 'I'm sorry to hear that.'

'He died when I was seven years old and

my mother left when I was eighteen. It was like she was waiting for me to be old enough so she could go, and she left me as soon as I moved out to university to study for my paramedic degree.'

'But you keep in touch with her?'

'Sporadic phone calls, but that's about it. It's hard to talk to her sometimes. She doesn't seem to hear anything I have to say. Always full of what's happening in *her* life. *Her* adventures. *Her* dramas.' She frowned. 'But what about your parents? You haven't really spoken about them much.'

'After my mum divorced my father, she got sick. She died after a long battle with multiple sclerosis. That's why I had to do everything for everyone. Mum couldn't if she was going through a bad phase, and as the oldest I kind of took charge. I had to.'

'Did you resent it?'

He shook his head. 'No. I'd do it all again. It brought me and my sisters really close together. We were a group. A band. We relied on one another, we looked out for one another, and we stuck together. Whenever one of us needs help, we call the others.'

'Is that how you ended up being at the birth of your nephew?'

He laughed, remembering. 'Yeah.'

'That must be nice, having such a close family. I can't imagine what that's like. Maybe you don't look for love because you already have it. With your sisters. I was an only child. Always alone.'

'Perhaps your mother acted the way she did because she couldn't handle losing her husband so suddenly and so young?'

Now it was Sophie's turn to frown. 'Maybe…'

'It must have been hard for her,' he said. 'Losing her husband and then having to look after a little girl when all she wanted to do was fall apart?'

'Maybe,' she said again.

She hadn't considered that. Not really. She'd just known that her dad had died and she'd got nothing from her mother in the way of comfort. In the way of attention. She'd felt starved of both from the get-go. Even before her dad had passed away.

'They were very much in love. I remember her telling me how much she loved him.'

'She must have been devastated, then. There's nothing worse than thinking that you have all this time with someone, only to discover that it's over before you know it. Your parents loved each other deeply. You had that. That's something. My parents were always distant. My father was hardly ever at home. When my mother divorced him it was almost a relief that he wasn't coming back, so that we could get on with our lives. Stop sitting there and waiting for someone to come home who didn't want to be there.'

She sighed. 'Families, eh? They sure know how to screw you over.'

And she couldn't get the thought out of her head that he was missing out on being with someone special. Someone as gorgeous and kind as he was. Why did he insist on being alone? He deserved to find someone special, even though it wouldn't be her.

'Maybe none of us know what we're doing...' He said. 'Stumbling our way through life, hoping we're making the right decisions. Once you have your daughter, you'll have that love you seek. It's already there—you're just waiting for her. Maybe even Connor will see the error of his ways.'

She laughed. 'I doubt that very much. And even if he did, would I want to know? He's already proved to be unreliable. I can't depend upon him the way your sisters depend on you.'

'You might feel differently afterwards. When the baby's here.'

Sophie doubted it very much. Connor had ruined his chance of being in a happy family with her and their daughter. But what would she do if he wanted shared custody or some contact? She'd have to give it to him, surely? What would that be like? Having to let her daughter go and spend time at her father's every week? Would he want her every weekend? Once a month? Never?

Perhaps she ought to find out if he'd even thought about this? Was it worth giving him a call? Was it worth reminding him that the time to change his mind was nearly at hand?

Just as she was about to think they might not have any more shouts that shift, the radio blared into life and Control told them they were needed at a road traffic accident.

She sighed. 'Would you like to do the honours?' she asked Theo.

He smiled and pressed the button for lights and sirens.

CHAPTER SEVEN

THAT WEEKEND, SOPHIE finally managed to get Connor on the phone. 'I was beginning to think you were ignoring my calls,' she said, rubbing at her swollen belly as the baby kicked frantically within her.

'Have you had it?' he asked abruptly.

It?

No *Hello, Soph, how are you?*

'Our daughter? Not yet.'

She tried not to sound angry. They needed to keep this civil. She didn't want her baby to pick up on the animosity that there was between the two of them. It wouldn't be fair. Their daughter was not a bargaining chip, or an asset to be passed around in a war. But she hated the fact that he'd used the word *it*. As if their baby was just some random object and not a precious, much wanted child.

'Then what do you want?'

'Well, I was hoping we could talk about things.'

'Like what?'

My God! Whatever did I see in this man? He used to be charming, right?

'About the future. About what's going to happen after the baby's born.'

'You mean money?'

'No, I don't mean money! Though I guess that will have to come into it sooner rather than later. I'm talking about when she's born—about if you'll want to see her and, if you do, what sort of contact you'd want.'

'I hadn't really thought about it.'

'Really?'

She couldn't believe this! Ever since they'd broken up, just over half a year ago, she'd thought of nothing else but this baby and she'd imagined—hoped—that beneath Connor's selfish exterior there might lurk a streak of love or a sense of duty towards the baby that he'd helped create.

He knew her due date. He'd stuck around long enough to find that out. Surely his mind had been drifting more and more to what would happen when his child was born? Or did he truly not care? How could she have once thought that this man cared for her? Was her radar so far off? Had she been so desperate for love that she'd taken his confidence, his swagger, his apparent ardent desire for her, as something else?

'It's been a difficult time for me, Sophie.'

'Difficult for *you*?'

'You wouldn't understand. I've had to make some huge adjustments since we broke up.'

'Since you walked away, you mean?'

There was a silence. Then, 'I'll pay child support. I spoke to my boss and he gave me a small pay rise after that deal I brokered, so paying maintenance shouldn't be a problem.'

'And will you want to see her?'

Another long silence. One so long she almost thought that maybe he'd put the phone down and walked away. But then she heard him let out a sigh.

'I don't know...'

'Well, you don't have long to figure it out. She's due in a couple of days, in case you've forgotten.'

'Of course I haven't!'

'Haven't you?'

Her anger seeped out. She couldn't help it. She was frustrated. Where was the man she'd thought she was in love with? And did she really want her beautiful daughter spending time with a man like him? She'd be better off spending time with Theo.

She felt strange, thinking that, then dismissed it. Hormones again. That was all. It was totally wrong even to think that Theo could be in any way shape or form a father to her child. Or even an influence. He simply wouldn't be around. He'd made it clear what he was to her. He hadn't even wanted to kiss her!

But…

I wish that he had. He's ten times the man Connor ever was. At least he's been honest with me from the start.

'I've got to go,' said Connor. 'I've an important call on the other line.' And he put the phone down.

Sophie threw her mobile phone across the room in frustration. An important call? Was she and the future of their daughter not important enough for him?

Boy! She'd royally screwed up with him.

Could she ever trust herself again to find a good man?

And did she even want to find one?

No.

Yes.

Perhaps they were all the same as each other?

But what about Theo?

What about him?

Her anger with Connor had burnt out any

real possibility that there was anything there. And why would she want it, anyway? *Why?*

And then the tears came. Floods of them, ripping through her like knives, and she sat on her couch, hiccupping her way through her breathing, as she wiped her nose on soggy tissues before throwing them across the room, to join her phone.

She didn't want to be wasting tears on Connor.

I'm not. I'm crying because I'm sad for my daughter.

The call to attend a pedestrian versus car came through, and Sophie got them to the accident site less than four minutes later.

Theo went to grab the jump bag and the Entonox as Sophie pushed her way through the milling crowd, all of whom seemed to be standing there, filming everything on their mobile phones.

He frowned. He was beginning to notice this more and more since working with Sophie, but this wasn't something they'd brought up in any of his lectures at university yet—how to deal with the general public, who often thought an accident was a good bit of footage to put on their social media sites.

He tried to ignore them, pushing through to get to their patient.

They found a little girl sitting in the road, crying, with a nasty laceration on her lower leg. The car driver stood next to them, crying her eyes out, obviously shocked and upset. She motioned to Sophie and Theo that she was fine and that they should check out the little girl first.

'Can you tell me what happened?' Sophie asked the woman holding the little girl's hand.

'I'm her mum. We were walking to school. Well, Keeley was skipping… As she got to the junction I shouted to her to stop. She turned… but she must have been too close to the edge and she fell backwards and hit the car.'

Theo was relieved. On the way to the job Sophie had told him that when calls came through like this, they had to assume the worst. That a pedestrian had been hit so hard by a vehicle that they'd been thrown into the air and over it. That injuries could be life-threatening. To get here and find that it was a low-speed impact and that this little girl hadn't been thrown anywhere was very reassuring.

'We're going to need some bandages,' Sophie said, pulling on her gloves. 'Hi, Keeley. My name is Sophie, this is Theo, and we're going to make you feel better, okay? Can I have a feel of your leg? You can stop me if anything hurts.'

Keeley continued to cry, but also nodded.

Theo watched carefully, noting how Sophie assessed the leg, her fingertips probing along the bones, checking her kneecap, her thigh, her foot. Checking for pedal pulses. Then she did the other leg.

'Did you bang your head, Keeley?' she asked.

'No.'

'I'm just going to check the rest of you, is that all right?'

Keeley was only sniffing by the time Sophie had finished doing her primary assessment.

'How is she?' asked Theo.

'I'm satisfied that the leg injury is the only problem.'

Theo passed her the bandages and she began to wrap the leg.

'You need to wrap the wound tight enough that it compresses the bleed, but not too tight that it damages the tissue beneath.'

He nodded. He knew about pressure bandaging. He'd applied it a couple of times in his life whilst serving in the army, waiting for medics. Stopping blood-loss could save a life. Lose too much and the body could go into shock.

Sometimes just the sight of their own blood could send a person into extreme shock. Thankfully, Keeley seemed made of stern stuff.

'You're being very brave, Keeley,' he said.

'Tell me what your favourite subject is at school.'

She sniffed and wiped her nose on her sleeve. 'PE. Netball.'

'What position do you play?'

'Centre.'

'Wow. You must be a really important player!'

Keeley smiled. He was so pleased to see the little girl smile he looked at Sophie, and caught her smiling, too.

'What else do you like doing?' he asked.

'I like baking. I want to be on that show on TV, but Mum says I'm not old enough.'

'Maybe try for the kids' version?'

Keeley nodded. 'Am I going to get stitches?'

He shrugged. The doctors at the hospital might stitch the wound, or they might choose to close it with glue. That wasn't his call, and he didn't know enough about it to say what the doctors would do once they'd had a better look at the wound and cleaned it. It would depend on how clean the edges were, how deep the injury was…whether anything beneath it had been damaged.

'Do you want stitches?' he asked.

Keeley shook her head. 'A cast would be cool, though.'

'So everyone can sign it?'

Keeley smiled again.

'Tell you what—let's put one of these on you.' He grabbed one of the gloves he kept in his pocket and put it on her hand, then he signed the back of it. 'Get people to sign that. I bet Sophie will sign it, too.'

Sophie did so—just as the ambulance arrived. As she handed over the case to the other paramedics, Theo stood to double-check on the driver of the car.

'What's your name?'

'Teresa. I saw her at the corner. I thought she'd stopped. But then she fell and…'

She burst into tears again and Theo rubbed at her shoulder to reassure her. 'Are you okay? Anything hurt?'

He saw the police arriving and waved them over. It probably had been a simple accident, but they'd need to take a statement, and most definitely would breathalyse this poor woman.

'I'm fine. I'm just…shaky.'

'The police will want to have a word with you, okay?'

She nodded. 'Absolutely. Whatever I can do to help.'

He left Teresa in their capable hands to go and say goodbye to Keeley before she was taken away. He clambered up into the ambulance and smiled at the little girl. 'Some people will do anything to get a day off school, huh?'

'Look, Theo!' she said. 'Danni and Neo have signed my glove, too!'

She held out her hand for him to see and he smiled at the smiley face one of the paramedics had drawn on her glove.

'Brilliant! You look after yourself, you hear?'

She nodded, and he waved her goodbye, stepping back out of the ambulance so that Keeley's mother could get in.

He found Sophie waiting for him. She had a broad smile upon her face.

'You did brilliantly back there, Theo. You really put her at ease. Went the extra mile. I'm very proud of you.'

'Thanks.' He smiled back at her, trying to be professional despite being inordinately pleased with her praise. He pulled his gaze away to watch the ambulance that carried Keeley drive away.

'You're good with kids, aren't you?' she said.

He shrugged. 'I try.'

'Your nieces and nephews are very lucky indeed.'

He looked back at her. Heard the wistfulness in her voice. Was she sad? Was she upset? Her smile had gone. She looked quite forlorn. Was she still worried about what kind of parent she'd be? He really didn't think she had anything to worry about. Clearly she wanted to be the best mother she could, and after seeing Sophie with her patients he couldn't imagine her being anything less than exemplary.

He wanted to tell her that. Pull her close and give her a hug. But look at what had nearly happened the last time he did.

Could he console her?

There was only one way to find out.

She needs a hug!

He reached out and pulled her in close against his chest, smiling when he heard her let out a long sigh and settle against him, her arms around his waist.

It felt *so good* to be held by Theo, his strong arms wrapped around her, holding her close. It was as if he was protecting her, keeping her safe, so that she could just relax for a few minutes and let someone else have the burden of worry.

Almost her entire life she'd felt as if she'd been looking after herself. Her dad dying when she was seven years old had changed everything. She'd loved her dad very much, and for him to just be there one day and not the next... gone...

It had been a massive heart attack, and he'd

been dead before he hit the floor, her mother had said. And her mother hadn't been much help to her afterwards, as she'd been grieving too.

Her mother had turned to other things to make her happy. Other people. Chasing the happiness she thought other people had, forgetting that she had a child who wanted more love than she was providing.

Sophie had just got on with being a little girl. Trying hard at school, working hard for herself, knowing that her mother was never that impressed with her grades, or her spelling test results, or how high she was on the reading ladder. She'd quickly learned that if she wanted to be happy then she would have to find happiness herself, the way her mother did, so she'd surrounded herself with good friends and made sure she had a good rapport with her teachers, who'd all liked her.

When Sophie had got older, and had been excited about going to university, her mother had announced that she would be going travelling and selling the house to pay for it. Sophie would need to find her own place to live at the end of her first term if she wanted to 'come home'.

It hadn't been a problem. In fact she'd been so self-sufficient by then it had almost been a relief that her mother had left, because she'd been worried about her. Her mum had been getting more and more depressed, saying that she felt stuck at home, having to be there to look after Sophie, and that she felt she needed to spread her wings and enjoy life before she got too old to enjoy anything.

Sophie had struggled to understand before, but since talking to Theo she'd begun to think that perhaps her mother hadn't been as bad as she remembered. Perhaps it had been just her mother's way of dealing with the loss of her beloved husband? Sophie knew a bit about loss. She had felt it when Connor had walked away without a backward glance. Okay, he hadn't died, but her dream of what her future might be had. Maybe she'd been too harsh on her mother? Maybe they had more similarities than she'd ever imagined?

Connor had swept Sophie off her feet, with his suave suits and expensive tastes, and he'd been so unlike anyone she'd ever known she'd fallen in love with him, thinking she'd finally found the one person who would stand by her side.

She had been hypnotised by his attention to her, his glamorous lifestyle…

And then he'd left, when life had got too hard. Too complicated.

By a child.

Her mother had been left alone just as suddenly. She'd been in shock. And maybe…just maybe…she'd looked outside herself to find the happiness she'd so desperately sought?

Had Sophie helped her with that? When her mother had pulled away, what had Sophie done? She'd tried to get her attention initially, but then she had just maintained that distance. Had helped it along by not really communicating with her mother. By standing alone.

Sophie knew how to look after herself. She'd been doing it for so long. Theo holding her like this, looking after her, well…it felt *good*! Even if it was only momentary.

'Six zero two? Are you clear of scene? Only we've got another job for you. Forty-two-year-old female entrapment, six minutes away from your current position.'

Control brought them back to reality and the radio blurting out was enough for them to break apart.

Guiltily, she smiled at Theo and then grabbed the radio. 'Yes, Control, we're clear of the previous scene. Show us as attending.'

She listened to the address carefully, already mapping out the route she'd need to take in her mind. 'Entrapment' could mean anything. What was the woman trapped under? Was she conscious? Was she bleeding?

'Pelican Place, Kings Road. Police, fire brigade and an ambulance crew also en route, six zero two.'

It was definitely something serious. And on the Kings Road… She knew that area. It was mostly housing. A new development was being built there. Was that Pelican Place? She'd driven past it a few times, but hadn't really had time to take in the name. If it was, then this could be a big job. Building sites were dangerous places.

'Call Control and ask them if HEMS is attending,' she told Theo, wanting to know if a doctor was going to be there.

But the helicopter was busy on another call.

Traffic was quite light as they raced to the job, and as soon as they arrived they were met by a foreman who was waiting with high-vis jackets and hard hats for them to wear.

'What's happened?' Sophie asked as she donned everything.

'We had the timber joists all set up for doing the roofs and… I don't know…they somehow came down without warning and trapped Annie.'

'Is she conscious?'

'Yeah, but she's in a lot of pain.'

No doubt.

The foreman led them through the site to their patient, who seemed to be trying to smile and joke through her pain with her colleagues, who were all gathered around.

Sophie turned to the foreman. 'The police, the fire brigade and an ambulance are on their way. Can you get someone to wait for them and lead them here?'

He nodded, and ordered a couple of guys to go and wait for support.

Sophie got down on her knees and smiled at Annie. 'Hi, Annie. I'm Sophie and this is Theo. How are you doing?'

She winced. 'My back hurts.'

In the distance, Sophie heard sirens. Good. Back-up would be here soon. They'd need help to lift these roof joists off Annie in a safe and controlled way. Her colleagues had done what they could, placing coats over her and trying to keep her warm. Shock frequently made a patient feel cold.

'And how's your breathing? Can you take deep breaths?'

Annie gave a little shake of her head. 'Think I might have cracked a rib or two...'

Theo had opened up the jump bag and was getting out the equipment. As soon as he heard Annie was having trouble taking big breaths he passed Sophie her stethoscope.

Placing the buds into her ears, she listened to Annie's chest. Both lungs sounded good, so she didn't think they had a punctured lung to worry about.

'Right, I'm just going to have a feel of your bones. If anything hurts you tell me and I'll stop, okay?'

'Okay.'

Sophie carried out a primary assessment and found no obvious breaks anywhere—though Annie did complain about a pain midway down her back where the main joist had hit her. Sophie was worried she had a fracture there. But it was good that Annie could still feel all four limbs and was able to wiggle her toes and move her hands. There didn't seem any risk of paralysis.

She looked up and saw the ambulance crew arrive, along with a small group of firefighters. She quickly apprised them of the situation and the fire crew set about working out how they were going to lift the joists off Annie without causing any more damage.

Annie was being a star. It had to be frightening to be in her position, and yet she was taking it like a champ. Laughing. Smiling. Not complaining. Sophie liked her a lot.

She managed to get a cannula into her arm and give her some morphine. 'That should keep you comfortable whilst we wait to get this wood off you.'

'What do you do, Annie? Are you a bricklayer?' Theo asked.

'Scaffolder.'

'You don't mind heights, then?'

'I love heights. Love climbing things.'

'Me too. I'm a rock-climbing instructor.'

Annie beamed. 'No way! What's your latest climb? I did Rainshadow last summer.'

'You did? Amazing! Sophie, we've got a real star here. Rainshadow at Malham Cove is one of the most difficult climbs in the UK. Even I haven't done that route yet.'

'Are you going to?' Annie asked, grimacing.

'I think I'm going to have to now. Got any tips for when I do?'

'Just take it steady, man. Enjoy every moment and conserve your strength. The end part at the summit takes everything from you.'

'Okay, I'll remember that.'

The fire crew had created a rope and pulley system that would safely lift the joists off Annie, and Sophie watched as Theo reached out to grab Annie's hand.

'We're not leaving you, okay?'

'Okay.'

Sophie smiled. He was so good with patients. He was going to make an amazing paramedic. One she would be glad to work with if he chose to stay in the south-central area.

Would he? She was enjoying seeing him every day. Enjoying being with him. To think of him going made her feel sad. She didn't like it. They hadn't spoken about his future yet. She had no idea what he planned to do when he qualified.

Maybe I haven't asked because I'm scared he'll say he's going?

With the joists lifted and the site secure enough for them to work in safety, Sophie, Theo and the other paramedics log-rolled Annie onto a spinal board and finally got a cervical collar around her neck.

The police got everyone to back away and give Annie some privacy as Sophie used scissors to cut off her clothes and check for any injuries that hadn't been seen when she was on her front, but it appeared that Annie had been lucky—if luck was what she'd had in the first place.

'Will she be okay?" asked the foreman.

'We'll know more when we get her to the hospital,' Sophie told him. But it was looking good to her, and she didn't think there was any chance of paralysis.

Theo and the fire crew helped carry Annie off the site to the ambulance. Sophie waddled after them, rubbing at her sore back and feeling glad to be standing up again as her knees were beginning to feel it.

They always told you that as a paramedic: *Don't kneel anywhere...you'll regret it.* Because sometimes there could be questionable stuff on the floor at people's homes and at accident sites. But sometimes it was impossible *not* to kneel.

Sophie recalled once, at the very beginning of her career, she'd forgotten this rule at the house of a drug addict, and when she'd knelt down next to the patient she'd knelt on a carpet wet with urine. Her colleague had laughed at her afterwards for her wet knee patches, and she'd had to change, but Sophie had just been glad it hadn't been a needle.

She'd remembered after that never to kneel again. But because of the pregnancy she'd been doing what she had to, to be safe as well as comfortable.

She winced and rubbed at her belly.

Theo frowned. 'Everything okay?'

'Yeah...just Braxton Hicks, I think.'

'Does it hurt?'

'No, it's just really tight. Uncomfortable.'

He nodded. 'Perhaps you need to take it easy? Sit down for a moment?'

'I'm fine. Just spent too long in one position, that's all. I need to loosen up.' She began to shake out her arms, wiggled her feet around.

'But you'll tell me if you need a minute?' he said.

She nodded. 'Of course!'

His concern for her was more than a little disconcerting. She didn't want to tell him that she was feeling a little bit of pain. Like cramping, quite low, beneath her bump. It couldn't be the start of anything, right? It had to be cramping from sitting in a weird position.

Him caring for her, holding her, hugging her, making her feel safe and protected—that was the dangerous thing! She was beginning to like it too much. Was starting to crave it. Having him be all concerned and trying to look after her was making her antsy, and if she wasn't careful she'd be falling for this guy hard.

Sophie got into the driving seat and yanked at the seatbelt irritably. Every day she seemed to need more and more belt! She was getting huge now, and totally understood why some women were fed up by the time they reached their due date.

And having a kind, caring hunk of a guy looking out for you when all you were used to was looking after yourself was *not* the kind of emotional trap she was looking to fall into right now!

CHAPTER EIGHT

SOPHIE OPENED THE contacts list on her phone and dialled the number she wanted. It rang for a brief while before being answered.

'Soph?'

Her mum's voice sounded so clear. Almost as if she were in the next room. And suddenly Sophie ached for her in a way she had never felt before. Her eyes filled with tears and she had to swallow hard to be able to talk.

The Theo effect in full action—making her *want*.

'Hi, Mum. How are you?'

Suddenly she wanted her close. Wanted to tell her everything. About Connor. About the baby.

'I'm doing just great! I haven't heard from you in a while.'

'No, I've had a lot going on.'

Pregnancy. Growing your grandchild.

How was she to tell her this? It would be so

out of the blue! Especially so close to her delivering. She regretted the distance between them, both geographically and emotionally. Had her mother simply taken the cue from her daughter that she wanted space, so stayed away? Barely called?

'Me too. Justin and I have just got back from a two-week holiday in the Algarve.'

'Justin?' She'd not heard that name mentioned before. And her mum had gone on holiday with him?

'Didn't I tell you about him? Oh, he's fabulous! Tall, dark and handsome. Works in the travel industry—so we're often flying here, there and everywhere. We went to Las Vegas a couple of months ago. I bet he could get you a good deal, if you and Connor want to go somewhere nice.'

Sophie sucked in a breath. This was the easy part.

Let's tackle this one piece of information at a time.

'Connor and I aren't together any more, Mum.'

There was a brief pause. 'Oh! Well, plenty more fish in the sea, eh? Look at me! Now, I've got to go. I'm getting ready for a meal out and I promised I wouldn't keep Justin waiting too long. You're doing okay, though?'

It was a rhetorical question. Not one that her mother expected her to answer in detail. Sophie could just imagine her mother's horror if she suddenly decided to say, *Well, actually, I'm not, because I'm pregnant and about to become a single mother*... and then launched into a massive diatribe about how alone she felt now. How she regretted their history. How she wished her life was different.

Sophie tried her hardest not to cry. Not to let tears fall or let her mother hear the upset in her voice. And suddenly she felt doubt about telling her. She just couldn't and she didn't know why.

'I'm fine.'

'All right, sweetie... Well, take care! Toodaloo!'

'Bye, Mum.'

But her mum had already rung off.

Now the tears came. The crying. It all just seemed too much. She was feeling so alone in the world. No mum, no dad, no Connor, no Theo. Just herself. Herself and her daughter.

Why am I always left on my own?

Was there something inherently wrong with her? Something unlovable that made people feel they didn't want to stick around? Even Theo had warned her about what he wanted from the very beginning—and what had she done? Fantasised about the guy and developed feelings for him, despite telling herself not to. It was as if she was punishing herself with people who weren't emotionally available. Why did she do that?

She decided that from this point on she wouldn't do it any more.

I'm going to live my life for me and my daughter and to hell with everybody else! If they can't be there for me, then I'll be there for me.

The silence in the house made her promise seem empty.

'What did *you* do at the weekend?'

Sophie was trying her hardest to ignore the cramping she was feeling. It had been coming on and off all morning, but she had a shift to do, and for some reason it made sense to her to ignore what might be happening.

She was thinking that if she could put off giving birth for just a few more days, then somehow she could make things right between her and Connor, so that their daughter would be loved deeply—though separately—by both of them.

'We went to a sports park and did some climbing,' Theo replied.

'We?'

Dammit, why did I ask that? It's none of my business who he spends time with.

'Some of the guys at the rock-climbing place.'

Guys. Men. Okay. So he hadn't spent time with any women.

Not that his personal life was any of her business. She shouldn't resent his freedom. Or was it more that she resented the fact that he was free of her? Another example of him living his life quite happily.

She reached into the middle compartment under the dashboard and brought out a string of red liquorice. She balled the whole thing up into one tight ball and popped it in her mouth. If she chewed, then she wouldn't say anything that might show her anger right now.

Sophie had woken up angry. Had woken up feeling that she was a different woman somehow.

She knew she had to take responsibility for the situation in life she found herself in. It was no one else's fault. She was the one who had made bad choices throughout, looking for love with men who weren't available. It might have something to do with her dad dying, and her abandonment afterwards by her mother, but if she wanted to be loved then she had to love herself first—and that meant a bit of tough love.

She'd given herself a stern talking-to, and now she was sitting there, trying not to count how long this pain was lasting, as in the distance there was a strange boom.

Sophie frowned and looked at Theo. Had he heard it?

Theo looked at her, his face full of concern. He had.

That boom hadn't been a good sound.

He glanced at Sophie and she grabbed the radio to contact Control.

'We're getting multiple calls coming through. Some kind of explosion at the Corn Exchange in Kingston.'

'Show us as attending.'

His mind whirled at what might have caused that noise. He hoped it wasn't a bomb. Control had said an explosion. Terrorism? Gas? No one knew. But he could hear Control summoning all available resources to the site, and he had no doubt that the police and the fire brigade were on their way, too.

He felt himself go into soldier mode. It was a certain mindset on a rescue mission. *Do what you can. Rescue those who can be saved. Come back later for the others.*

He had no doubt that whatever they were driving towards, it was going to be a big job.

A turning point in his life that he would never forget.

Beside him in the car, Sophie drove intently, one hand rubbing at her underbelly.

'Baby kicking?' he asked.

'Um…yeah.'

He frowned, worrying about her. She'd been odd since the weekend, and he'd been noticing more and more that she was feeling discomfort as she got closer and closer to her due date.

'You know, no one would think less of you if you stood back from this.'

'Why would I be standing back?' she asked tersely.

He sighed. 'You're heavily pregnant, Soph. This could be dangerous.'

'It's dangerous for everyone—and besides, I'm fine. You don't have to look out for me, okay?'

Had something happened at the weekend? Had she realised how her world was going to change? How she was no longer going to be just Sophie, paramedic, but Sophie, *mother*? Perhaps she was still worrying about whether she'd be able to do it?

He figured that might be it. She hadn't been a mother before and, from what he understood, her own mother hadn't exactly been an exemplary model. He knew what it meant to be alone. To raise yourself. How you became dependent upon yourself and made your own decisions. Sometimes that could make you a little *too* independent. Made you snippy with people who tried to help.

But everyone winged it as first-time parents. Babies didn't come with a manual—you went on instinct. And generally people tried to help you.

Traffic was building as they got closer and closer to the town centre, and sometimes the lights and sirens weren't enough to clear a way through the streets. Sophie had wound down her window and was waving at people to get out of the way. At one point they found themselves stuck, with literally no place to manoeuvre, and Sophie cursed and swore, using words he'd never heard her use before.

He got out of the car and ran to the front of the traffic that was stopped at a red light, where he began to instruct everyone where to move to. Slowly but surely he created a narrow lane for the car to drive down, and Sophie stopped to collect him.

'Thanks.'

'No problem.'

They raced forward again, then hit another load of traffic. He could now see people moving away in their hordes from the city centre, which was was filled with a mix of dust and smoke.

Sophie parked where she thought it was safe and they both got out and began to run as fast as they could towards the Corn Exchange. Theo was faster than her but he stayed with her, constantly looking back as she tried to run, holding her belly before her.

The building looked as if it had exploded outwards. There was glass everywhere, tables and chairs from the coffee shop strewn all over the pavement, and one or two people sitting there in shock, some with dirt and blood trickling down their faces. A lone teddy bear lay discarded in the middle of the road.

'Theo.' Sophie pointed to indicate that he should help those he could see and get them away from the Corn Exchange in case there was a second blast.

He passed her the smaller jump bag, so that she would have supplies to treat patients, and then ran towards the first person he saw: a woman with long dark curly hair and a laceration to her face from the hairline down to her eyebrow.

'Let me help you—let me take a look.' He knelt beside her and took her hand in his and gave it a squeeze. 'You're okay. I've got you. Do you know what happened?'

'I… I don't… I was sitting having coffee. I was working on my— Oh! My laptop!' She turned to try and find it, tried to get up and look for it.

Theo kept her in a seated position on the kerb. 'Don't worry about that for now. It can wait. Let's get you sorted.'

As he got bandages and saline to wash the wound from his jump bag he glanced around him, saw Sophie attending to a man whose arm she was putting into a sling.

He glanced back at his own patient. 'What's your name?'

'Gemma.'

'Hi, Gemma. I'm Theo.'

She managed a weak smile at him. 'Am I bleeding?'

Gemma was clearly in shock. A lot of these people were going to be.

In the distance he heard the very welcome sound of more sirens. That was good. They were going to need a lot of extra hands here—a lot of ambulances. There were so many people with cuts and injuries, and there might be people trapped inside with more serious wounds. No one had any idea of what had caused the explosion, or if there was any danger of another one. They'd need the police and the fire brigade to secure the area.

Gemma's wound was jagged and deep. After cleaning it with saline, Theo applied a pressure bandage around her head and helped her walk further away from the Corn Exchange.

He sat her down on the ground near their vehicle. 'I want you to wait here, okay? Don't move and don't go looking for your laptop—it's not important.'

'Where are you going?'

'I've got to help the others.'

She nodded, understanding. 'Okay.'

He ran back towards the scene, eyes scanning quickly, trying to judge who needed him the most, and afraid that his skills would not be up to par for what might be needed from him. But it was all hands on deck, so he figured his basic skills would have to do. Besides, reinforcements were on their way.

He spotted a man with a little boy. He was trying to pick a shard of glass out of the child's leg.

'Stop!' he called out, running over.

The shard was large, and he had no idea how much was embedded. It could just be the tip—but what if it was something more? If this piece of glass had torn through an artery, then the little boy could bleed out.

The man faltered and looked up. 'But he's hurt!'

'I know—but if you pull that out it could make it a lot worse.'

The little boy was strangely quiet. Shock.

'What's his name?' asked Theo.

'Kyle.'

'Okay, Kyle.' Theo knelt to face him, tilted his chin up with his finger so that Kyle would look at him and meet his eyes. 'I'm Theo, and I need you to listen to me, okay?'

The boy stared back, saying nothing, his eyes blank.

'We're going to have to leave that in until we get you to hospital and do a scan or an X-ray. So I'm going to wrap a bandage *around* the glass, but I don't want you to touch it or move it, okay?'

He was really concerned. There wasn't much blood around the wound. If the glass was tamped down on an artery Kyle could bleed out in seconds.

'Were you outside the coffee shop?' he asked the father.

The man nodded.

'What happened?'

'I don't know. One minute we were sitting there, enjoying our drinks, the next—*boom*—we were being thrown into the road.'

Theo wrapped Kyle's leg and glanced around him to see what Sophie was up to. He couldn't see her from where he squatted on the pavement, but behind him he saw other emergency vehicles arriving, paramedics and firefighters running in all directions, and he felt a swell of relief.

Standing, he waved over to the first ambulance and headed over to the paramedic. It was Ross. 'Hey, man. We've got an injury here, and another woman with a facial laceration over by our vehicle.'

'Okay.'

'Sophie is…' Theo looked around and caught a glimpse of green uniform disappearing into the building behind a team of firefighters.

He swore, grabbed his equipment bag, and broke into a run.

'Soph!'

Theo's voice right behind her reassured her.

'Theo. There's a young woman over there who needs help. Looks like facial lacs, maybe some embedded glass—can you get her out?'

He looked about for the woman and began scrambling over the rubble and broken glass to get to the patient. 'What are you going to do?' he asked.

'I think I heard something. A child. A cry from back there.' She pointed to a doorway that led further into the building.

Beyond all the other noise—the coughing, the crying, the hubbub from the observers who'd been beginning to gather—she alone had heard the noise as the firefighters beside her had clambered over rubble in their breathing equipment.

And it was a noise that had called to her.

The cry of a baby.

Medical back-up would be coming—she could hear the reassuring sounds of sirens fighting their way through the streets of this town. She had Theo with her, the fire crew. All she had to do was quickly run in, grab the baby, and she'd be out again in a matter of seconds.

She would be saving a life. She couldn't leave a baby in there. It could be hurt. *It could be dying.* It hadn't even started to live yet!

'Be quick,' Theo said, giving her a look as he helped the stunned young woman to her feet and began to guide her out.

She nodded, her feet already beginning to carry her forward, waddling in the fastest run she could do in her condition. She felt another cramp coming on and winced. She'd had one earlier in the car and had thought it was maybe because she was sitting in a funny position. This one had to be because of all the adrenaline filling her—and even if it was something else, she would have plenty of time to go and find one of the other paramedics and tell them once she was out of there…

It could be something else.

Braxton Hicks weren't meant to be painful and these cramps were.

She had to be in labour.

Sophie clambered over a splintered broken table to get inside, her eyes adjusting to the dark, dusty interior. The coffee shop was in complete disarray. Almost destroyed. There were chairs everywhere, broken china cups and plates on every surface, and yet, strangely, a cake sat on a counter completely whole, its icing accompanied by debris from the roof.

She coughed, feeling the dust in the back of her throat. 'Hello?'

The crying continued. It was coming from the back. There were abandoned coats and boxes which she had to climb past, getting closer and closer to the crying, and finally finding the source of the noise. A baby in a pushchair, still strapped in and completely unharmed. It was probably crying because of the noise of the explosion. Or because it wanted to be picked up. It must be terrified. Was the mother the woman that Theo was helping?

'Sophie! Have you found anything?'

Theo's voice, right behind her, had her picking up the baby and turning around with her in her arms. 'Yes!'

'Give her to me. Let's go.'

She passed the baby over to him, wincing as another pain came and clutching at her abdomen.

'We need to get out of here. Come on!' He held out his spare hand.

'You take her out, get her checked. I'll be right behind you.'

He nodded and began to make his way through the mess and out of the café.

Sophie took a moment to breathe through her contraction, putting her hands on her knees for support. It completely took her breath away, the pain enveloping her entire abdomen so that she couldn't move. Couldn't follow Theo and the baby.

She stood upright again when it was over, relieved, and even smiled at herself. It was happening. The baby was coming. She was going to be a mother!

She took a step forward, and then saw smoke beginning to issue from a back room. Something was burning. She could hear it. A crackling noise.

'Guys?' she called out, hoping one of the firefighters was close enough for her to signal to.

As she started to walk out through the coffee shop, she noticed a storeroom of some kind. There were some canisters there. They were right next to the flames.

Gas? She didn't know, and she didn't have time to react. She turned, wanting to run, wanting to tell the firefighters that there was a dangerous area to secure—and then there was another loud boom and something knocked her off her feet. The ground disappeared and she fell into a deep, dark hole, landing awkwardly, feeling a pain shooting up her leg before she passed out.

Theo had just handed the baby to a paramedic when behind him there was another explosion. He covered the baby and the paramedic with his own body, then turned around, looking for Sophie.

Had she got out?

She'd been right behind him!

'Soph...? *Sophie!*'

He ran back towards the Corn Exchange, but the firefighter coming out of the building held him back. 'You can't go back in there.'

'My colleague's in there!'

'We need to make sure this building is secure.'

'She's heavily pregnant! She was right be-hind me!'

The firefighter looked grim. 'Okay. I think I saw her before the second explosion. But *we* go first—understand?'

Theo nodded. He thought the second explosion had seemed smaller than the first. Or was that just wishful thinking? He could kick himself for not checking that Sophie was following him, but he'd been in such a rush to get out of there, to get the baby some proper help, that he'd assumed...

Never assume! Always check! Hadn't his corporal told him that?

Theo looked despairingly at the building. If something had happened to Sophie he'd never forgive himself.

It took every ounce of self-control he had not to follow the firefighters in, and when they came back out empty-handed the lump in his throat almost threatened to stop him from breathing.

The fire chief came over to him. 'Okay, we've found her, but she's trapped.'

'Is she all right?'

'She says she's fine, but her leg is caught under some concrete and she thinks it's broken. She's asking for Theo.'

His heart sank and he felt sick. 'That's me.'

'The floor's collapsed and she's fallen through to a room below. We'll need to secure the safety of the floor before we let anyone in.'

'Let me down there. I'm a rock-climber, an ex-soldier. She knows me, and she can tell me what to do when I get down there with some equipment.'

'There's a doctor on his way via helicopter, isn't there?'

'But he's not here—and I am! Please! You said she asked for me.'

The fire chief seemed to think about it. 'All right, seeing as she wants you. We'll give you the equipment to help free her leg, so you can splint it.'

He nodded, glad to finally be of use, to put right this wrong and help Sophie—bring her to safety as he should have done after he'd helped the baby. He'd never forgive himself if he didn't do this.

It was his fault for leaving her behind.

Down in the dusty dark, Sophie tried not to cry or feel alone. She seemed to be in some sort of basement under the coffee shop. She'd landed on the floor and her right leg was trapped beneath a slab of concrete wall. It hurt badly, but it was nothing compared to the intense contractions she was experiencing. And—she glanced down, wincing—her waters had just broken.

I can't give birth down here! Not like this!

This was not the way she'd planned on bringing her daughter into the world! She'd pictured a beautiful clean, white hospital room. Some music playing. Soft lighting. Maybe even in a birthing pool! Candles. Someone mopping her brow. Midwives softly coaching her through contractions. Gas and air…

Not *this*. Not this dirty, dusty basement with a hole in the roof above her and smoke and rubble all around! With the stench of dirt and stone and cloying smoke.

Not alone. Never alone. I deserve more! Goddamn it, I deserve better than this!

'Sophie?'

Her heart almost stopped in joy at hearing his disembodied voice above her. 'Theo?'

'It's me. I'm coming down.'

'Be careful!'

'I've got an entire fire crew making sure I am.'

She looked up and saw him being lowered down through the small gap, climbing ropes and pulleys attached to his waist and hips. Carabiners held bags of equipment below him as he descended, and as he got closer and closer towards her, she began to cry.

'Oh, Theo!'

'I'm down!' he called to the firefighters above, unclipping himself and all the equipment. Then he went over to her, knelt down and wrapped his arms around her. 'Sophie!' He pulled back, frowning, looking down at the wetness around his knees.

'I'm in labour, Theo. My waters have broken.'

He looked grim. 'Okay…we're gonna get you out. We have time. You've not had any contractions yet, right?'

She nodded, biting her lip. Feeling guilty. 'One or two.'

'Sophie!' he admonished her. 'How many? How often?'

'I've not been counting. But I've had them all morning and they appear to be coming every few minutes.' Then she looked at her leg and winced. 'I'm also trapped.'

'I've got stuff to get you out. A jack to help lift the concrete so we can free you. And then we're going to haul you up out of here.'

'Have they got a pulley strong enough?' She smiled, trying to joke. She wanted to be brave. Like Annie had been, trapped beneath those roof joists, joking to her colleagues.

'For a little ole thing like you?' He smiled back and began pulling the equipment out of the bag the fire crew had given him. One piece was like a car jack, and he wedged it beneath the slab of concrete that was pinning her lower leg.

'I think I've broken my tib and fib.'

'You might not have, though.'

'I can feel it, Theo. Even if the fall didn't break it, the wall crushing it certainly did. And what about compartment syndrome?'

Theo shook his head. But she knew that compartment syndrome was a condition in which increased pressure could build up in an affected part of the body, resulting in insufficient blood supply to the tissues.

'You've not been trapped long enough for that, have you?' he asked.

She nodded. 'It's a crush injury—'

And then another contraction came, and she had to close her eyes and breathe through it. She felt Theo take her hand, could feel his thumb caressing the back of it, hear his soothing words coaching her through her breathing. His strength, his presence, helped her.

When it was over, she opened her eyes again and smiled at him. 'I'm glad you're here.'

'I'd like to say, *Me too*, but—' he looked around them '—I can think of better places we could be doing this.'

His radio crackled into life with a disembodied voice. 'How are you doing down there?'

Theo depressed the button on the radio with his thumb. 'We're okay.'

'We've got everything stable up here, so whenever you're ready…'

'Thanks.'

Another contraction hit, this one much stronger, and Sophie stared at Theo in shock as she felt the urge to push. *What?* This couldn't be happening! Already? Most first-time mothers took hours and hours, if not days, in labour.

'Theo, I think I need to—' Her voice was cut off by the primal groan that issued from her throat and she couldn't help it—she bore down.

'Sophie? I need you to look at me, okay?'

She opened her eyes, fear flooding her body, panic encroaching fast. She was stuck underground, her leg trapped, possibly broken, and her baby was trying to come into the world at the same time. This shouldn't be happening. Not this quickly. Not here. Not in this terrible place!

'If you're going to push, then I'm going to need to see what's going on.'

She shook her head. Not because she didn't want him to look, but because she couldn't believe this was happening. 'I'm scared!'

'I know you are. But I'm here, and I know

what to do. We're going to get you out of this—
do you hear me?'

He reached into the bag for scissors. She
knew that with her leg trapped there was no
way he was going to get her trousers off eas-
ily. He cut through the fabric from the ankle
all the way up her leg to her hips, including her
underwear, and clicked on the radio.

'I'm going to need someone to send down a
couple of blankets, stat.'

'Will do. Is she going into shock?'

'She's about to give birth.'

Another contraction hit and Sophie sucked
in a huge lungful of the dusty, dirty air and
bore down as much as she could. The pushing
helped. It somehow helped to push the pain
away, made the pain a useful tool rather than
something to be endured.

When it was over, she looked at Theo in ex-
haustion.

'I can see the baby's head. She's got hair.'

Sophie wanted to smile, but another contraction was coming and she had to deal with that.

Beside her, Theo stood and caught the blankets that were being passed down, and when
her contraction was over he got her to lift her
bottom so that he could place one clean blanket
beneath her and one above her, over her groin.

She felt better about that. There would be

some dignity, at least. Something was clean. Her baby wouldn't slither out onto a cold, concrete floor, but would instead feel softness.

'Soph, the next bit is going to hurt. I think you're going to crown with the next contraction or so…so when you feel that burn, you push through it—okay?'

She nodded. 'I forgot you've done this before. You delivered a baby. Your sister's.'

'Little Leo. But I hardly delivered him. I just stayed up by Martha's head and let her crush my fingers.'

'Leo and Theo.' She breathed in, smiling, resting her head against the wall behind her. 'I'm glad I'm not calling my daughter Cleo.'

He smiled and nodded. 'What a family we'd make, eh?'

She looked at him then. She thought he seemed to want to say something else, but then another contraction began.

Sophie sucked in the biggest lungful of air that she could and pushed down into her bottom. She could feel her baby moving through her. It felt as if she was pushing all the bones in her pelvis out of place, as if her skin was stretching so thin it would tear, and she cried out.

'Sophie, just pant! Pant it out! That's it.

That's perfect. Okay, her head's out. Do you want to feel her?'

She reached down and—oh! She could feel her! Her daughter! It was nearly over.

'One more push, one more...'

When the pain came again she pushed as hard as she could and gasped as her daughter slithered out into Theo's waiting hands.

He scooped her up and placed her on Sophie's belly, draping her in a blanket and rubbing the baby's back, as her child burst into lusty cries.

Above, she heard clapping and cheering and yells of congratulation, and she cried as she wrapped her hands around her baby and bent to kiss her head. She did have hair! Lots and lots of dark hair. And she looked a good size, too.

'Well done, Soph,' Theo said, clamping the cord with two scissor clamps, then cutting it.

She couldn't believe it! She'd done it. Her baby was here and she was perfect. She checked everything—ten fingers, ten toes. Then she hurried to undo her uniform top and held her daughter skin to skin, not caring about anything else. She felt as if she could stay there all day, just holding her and watching her. The broken, blown-out basement room was forgotten.

Theo was smiling at them both. There was something in his eyes that she couldn't understand, but she didn't try to. All her thoughts were on her beautiful baby daughter. They needed to get out of here.

Then Theo turned, glanced at her leg. 'Soph…? I've still got to free that leg.'

She nodded. 'Okay.'

'It's gonna hurt.'

She knew that. But right there and then she felt as if she could get through anything. 'Just do it.'

He nodded.

Sophie held her daughter tight and used every ounce of her inner strength to breathe as she felt him wedge the jack under the concrete slab. He glanced at her once last time, to make sure she was ready, and she nodded. He began—and as the concrete was lifted and her mangled leg was revealed she almost passed out from the pain.

CHAPTER NINE

SOPHIE LAY IN her wonderfully clean hospital bed, in a room that contained no dust, no smoke, no rubble, and truly felt blessed. Her daughter was healthy and perfect.

The doctors wanted to keep them both in for a while—not only to make sure neither of them had picked up any infection from the dirty basement, but also to let her leg heal after the lengthy surgery she'd had to put in a plate and screw back together the comminuted fractures of her lower leg bones. Both her tib and fib *had* been broken, although thankfully neither of the breaks had gone through the skin.

She'd had surgery and given birth and now she needed to rest, and she was looking forward to bonding with her daughter Cassidy.

Leaning over her cot, Sophie tried to work out who her daughter looked like. She'd read somewhere that babies tended to look like their fathers right after birth, to help the male parent bond with his child, but the only thing on Cassidy's face that looked even a little like Connor was her nose, and a little around her eyes. Everything else looked like Sophie as a baby. At least in the photos she'd seen of herself.

Cassidy made a small mewing sound in her sleep and Sophie smiled, aching to pick her up again and hold her in her arms. But she knew, as an only parent, that she did not want to create a rod for her own back if she taught Cassidy that she would be picked up every time she made a cute sound.

Instead, Sophie lay back against her pillows and looked out of the hospital window. She could see brown trees and green grass, and those colours had never looked more beautiful. She supposed she ought to call her mother and let her know about Cassidy.

She'd not even had the nerve to tell her she was pregnant! But she couldn't let her mum live without knowing that she was a grandmother. Who knew? It might make her come and visit. She hadn't seen her mother in ages…

And she supposed, reluctantly, that she ought to tell Connor. He deserved to know his child had been born, even if he didn't care for either of them.

But the person she longed for the most was Theo.

Where was he?

The doctors had told her that he had remained by Cassidy's bedside for hours, watching over her whilst Sophie was in surgery, and that he'd wanted to wait by her side in Recovery afterwards too, but the nurses had sent him home to get some sleep, eat and change his clothes.

She felt she had so much to say to him. She wouldn't be able to express enough in words to thank him for looking after her and standing guard over Cassidy, whilst Sophie could not. How could she ever thank him enough for that?

She knew that he hadn't wanted to watch over anyone else's children ever again. That he was a free spirit. And she wanted to be able to say that she knew that before he vanished from her life for good.

Because she certainly wouldn't hold him to that *friends for at least a year* promise he'd made in jest. It wasn't fair on him—not when she knew he didn't want this, or anything she had to offer him. It would be unfair of her to expect him to want her because of what they'd been through together.

He'd helped her give birth. Had delivered Cassidy safely. She would always remember him with fondness even if he did walk away from them both.

And yet the thing she feared the most was that he wouldn't show. What if she never saw him again? What if he figured he'd done his part?

The ambulance service would probably place him with another mentor to finish off the last few days of his placement and he'd be busy, he'd forget her, and…

Sophie wiped away a stray tear.

I have to let him go.

If you love someone, let them go—wasn't that what they said? Whoever *'they'* were. You let them go. You put their needs above your own because you loved them. Because that was what love was about. Being selfless.

Theo had done it with his sisters, hadn't he? He'd let them leave the nest and find partners and leave him behind because he'd wanted them to have happiness. He'd always wanted them to have happiness—it was why he had cared for them when his mother had got sick.

If you love someone…

Did she love Theo?

I guess in a way I do. Probably for all the wrong reasons—but that's just me falling for the wrong guy again.

It was time to stand on her own two feet and be the mother that Cassidy needed. To fully focus on her daughter and not have her heart fretting and yearning for a man it couldn't have.

Why do I even think I want Theo, anyway? Just because he's kind? Because he makes me laugh? Because he's brave and strong? Because he makes me feel good? Because he protected my child when I couldn't? Because he brought her into the world? Because I suddenly can't imagine my life without knowing I can talk to him whenever I want to?

'Damn it!'

Sophie reached out to the box of tissues at the side of her hospital bed and dabbed at her eyes before wiping her nose. Sensing her distress, Cassidy began to awaken, her face pulling into a pout, before earnest crying began.

Sophie bent at the waist to reach out and lift her up into her arms. Glancing at the time, she saw that Cassidy was due for her next feed, so she unbuttoned her top and offered Cassidy her breast. The baby latched on almost instantly and began to suck. It felt strange, but beautiful and natural. She felt as if she was doing the one thing she'd always wanted to do. Being a mother.

She took the time to appreciate everything about her daughter. Her fluffy dark hair, the softness of her skin, the lashes resting upon her chubby cheeks, the shape of her lips. How gorgeous she was, and how much she loved her already.

Could I love anyone else as much as I do her?

Probably not.

But she knew of someone who came really close to deserving that level of love…

Knowing that he was never to be hers, she pushed the image of Theo's face out of her mind and focused on what mattered right now.

Her beautiful daughter.

His first thought upon waking was, *How many hours have I been asleep?*

Theo checked his mobile phone and saw that it was just gone eight o'clock in the morning, so he must have slept for a good eight hours. And he'd needed it after yesterday.

He'd spent so long living off adrenaline after the blasts, taking care of the casualties, running after Sophie into that devastation and finding her trapped, helping her deliver her baby girl…

He smiled to himself as he thought of that beautiful baby girl and the look on Sophie's face when he'd handed her daughter to her.

That was love. Pure love.

And he'd been envious.

He'd felt the same way at Leo's birth. Watching Martha take her son in her arms, seeing that love in her eyes, that connection they instantly had and knowing that it wasn't his, knowing it wasn't something he could be part of.

It had been a shocking emotion for him to acknowledge.

And he had feelings for Sophie, whether he liked to admit them or not. He'd found himself thinking of what it might be like to be with someone like her. He admired her. Her strength, her skill, her intelligence, her determination. The way she cared for people.

And he was most definitely attracted to her.

To see her on that concrete floor, rubble and devastation all around her, sitting there holding her newborn daughter in her arms... He'd wanted to sit beside her, drape his arm around her shoulder and just hold them both. Be part of it. Be part of something bigger than himself.

He'd felt envious of the adventure they were about to go on as a new family, and had known he would be left behind. He'd watched over his sisters and had to let them go when they'd found partners and had children of their own. Now he would have to do the same with Sophie.

I almost felt like the proud father myself.

But that wasn't what he wanted. A family... Or was it?

Sophie had asked him once what he would do if he found true love and he'd not known the answer. Right now, he'd probably want to grab it with both hands—but he couldn't do that with Sophie. She wasn't his. Would never be his. She had a baby now. Had other priorities. She would put her daughter first in all things. And there was a father lurking in the dark shadows who hadn't played his hand yet, either. Theo knew he would play it at some point.

Knowing Sophie—being with her, talking to her—had made him realise that he had always defined himself in the past by what he could be to others. Whatever they'd needed from him, he had given it. After his sisters had left, he had decided to take the time to find out who he was by joining the army. He'd thought it would put him through tests and trials and make him who he was meant to be—but he'd just found himself giving to his army family, too.

Was that what he was really meant to be?

Part of something bigger than what he was alone?

He'd tried to stand alone. Had forced it to happen many times—leaving Jen being one of those occasions. He'd needed it. To discover who he was, what he was, and what he wanted.

Was that Sophie?

This was playing with his head. He'd behaved a certain way for so long…to suddenly have these different thoughts, ideas and wants was confusing. Because if he did want Sophie and her baby, what was he to do? It was one thing to look after his little sisters—he was related to them through blood, after all—but totally another to take on another man's child.

And yet when he'd looked down at Sophie's daughter he'd felt something. Happiness. Pride. Love.

He knew he was capable of love, but was he capable of maintaining it? His own father hadn't managed it, and Theo had kept all his relationships short on purpose—not wanting to commit, not wanting to go with the flow, because he was afraid. There were no certainties with relationships. How many did he know that had problems? Too many. How many successful relationships had he seen?

And yet people still got into relationships all the time—and not just simple ones. Complicated ones. Because they had the hope and the belief that they could make it through whatever was to come.

Theo was a man who had climbed rock faces, conquered mountains, run towards gunfire and exploding buildings. He tried. He worked hard. And most of all he didn't like letting people down. He didn't like leaving people behind.

He never wanted to be anything like his father, so it was easier not to even try to be one. Why tempt fate when there were no certainties?

He thought again of how Sophie had looked with her baby. How he had felt looking at them…how much he had wanted to be a part of their little family.

He could have that one day.

If he was brave enough.

But not with Soph. Not right now, anyway.

She had her relationship to sort out with Connor.

Theo threw off his bedclothes. He would take a shower, grab a bite to eat, and then he would go and visit Sophie and her baby girl in hospital. Make sure they were okay. See if there was anything she needed.

She'd need help in these early days, what with her leg and everything. He'd help her out. Do what he could. And when she got more mobile, he'd start to take steps back. Give her space. Let her live her life.

So why does the idea of stepping back feel so wrong?

'A *grandmother*?'

Her mother's shock reverberated down the phone.

'Are you sure?'

Sophie laughed. 'Well, there's a beautiful

baby girl in my arms, so...yeah, I am. And you are a grandmother. I'm sorry I didn't tell you before...everything was just mixed up and crazy. I didn't even want to tell you that Connor and I had broken up.'

'Well... I don't know what to say. What are you going to call her?'

'Cassidy.'

'Oh, I like that.'

Sophie smiled. 'Good.'

She'd wanted her mother to know so badly, and now that she did she wanted her mother to want to see them. To say that she would come and see them both. Visit. Look after them for a bit whilst she got over the birth and the surgery.

Wasn't that what mothers did? Came to cook or clean or fold laundry whilst the new mother and her baby got to know one another? It would be nice not to go back to an empty home. Nice to think that maybe, just this one time, her mother would do the kind of thing that mothers normally did.

But she knew her mother. And since talking to Theo she had begun to see what had happened in the past in a different light. They'd both been grieving. Both had coped with the death of a father and a husband in different ways.

'I would love you to see her, Mum. I've been

thinking about how things have been between us in the past and I want to rectify that. Maybe you could come visit? What with the broken leg and everything, I'm going to need an extra pair of hands…'

It was worth asking, wasn't it? She never knew—her mum might change.

'I can't, Soph. I've got responsibilities here.'

Her mother sounded sad to be saying no and Sophie nodded silently, trying to understand. But with all the hormones surging around her body she found herself trying not to cry. She understood. But she also wanted her mum with her so badly! She wanted her to put her arms around her and hold her close and tell her how proud she was of her! She'd hoped they might take this opportunity to get to know one another again and grow closer, now that Sophie had had time to think about all they had gone through.

'I've got so much on my plate here. There are people here I can't let down.'

'I understand. It's fine…honestly. I'll send you some photos.' Sophie wiped her eyes with her hospital gown.

'That'll be great—and I'll get to see her sometime. It's not like she's going to go away, is she? When I'm free again…maybe nearer Christmas… I'll try and get down to you both.'

'Great. We'd love to have you for Christmas. Bring Justin. It would be nice to meet him.'

'I'd love that. And I'd love to get to know you again. You and I…we messed up, didn't we?'

Sophie nodded, saying nothing.

'I love you, kiddo. I'll see you soon, okay? Bye!' and then she rang off.

Sophie held the phone in her hand, wondering how on earth she was going to cope at home if she had no one to help her whilst she hobbled around on crutches. Taking care of a newborn would be hard enough, but to deal with a broken leg, too…? Would they even let her leave the hospital unless she could prove she had support?

She hoped her mother would come to mend things between them. They'd mentioned it briefly. Both acknowledged it. Perhaps that had been the problem all along? Neither of them had been able to admit there was a problem, but until they did, they couldn't fix anything.

But now she felt she understood her mother a little more. Her mum had been lonely. Grief had left her alone and looking at a child who had her father's eyes. It must have been difficult. She'd loved Sophie's dad very much. And she'd spent the rest of her life chasing love, trying to find it with others. And she'd done it without Sophie.

Maybe that had been the wrong way to do it, but now, with both of them willing to try and fix things, at the right pace for them both, then maybe they had a chance at the kind of relationship Sophie had always hoped for.

It took Theo ages to find a parking spot. He found himself wishing he had the rapid response vehicle, so he could park anywhere and not spend twenty-five minutes driving up and down the rows of cars, waiting for someone to pull out so he could quickly nip in. Not to mention the outrageous parking fee he'd have to pay when he finally emerged from the hospital again—but he wasn't going to let that worry him too much.

He hoped Sophie would be awake when he got to her room. The last time he'd seen her she'd just come out of surgery, and she'd looked so small in that bed, so vulnerable, he'd felt a pain in his chest. When the nurse had suggested he go home to take a break, and said she'd keep an eye on Cassidy until Sophie woke, he'd accepted. Gladly. The strange feelings assailing him had not been making sense at all.

He buzzed the door at the unit and spoke over the intercom, telling them who he was there to see. Like a shield, he held a box of chocolates and a teddy front of him as he headed to Sophie's room. Peering through the window, he saw that she was awake, sitting up in bed, with one hand upon her daughter as she slept.

A huge smile crept across his face. He gave a quick knock and then pushed the door open. 'Room for one more?'

'Theo!' Sophie beamed at seeing him, and he headed in and placed the gifts beside her, not knowing whether he ought to kiss her on the cheek or not. He made the sudden decision to do it anyway, but kept it brief, telling himself not to do anything stupid like breathe her in, or anything like that.

'How are you feeling?' he asked, sitting down.

She shrugged. 'Bit rough. But I think that's the anaesthetic. They said I might feel sleepy for a day or so.'

'How's the leg?'

'Fixed.'

He nodded. 'And Cassidy?'

Sophie smiled. 'She's wonderful. Do you want to hold her?'

He wanted to—very much—but every time he had before, when Sophie had been in surgery, he'd found himself imagining what it would be like if she were his.

'Oh, I don't think I should—'

'You delivered her. You should at least have

the honour of giving her a cuddle after coming to our rescue.'

Theo got up from his seat at the side of the bed and walked round to Cassidy's cot. Cassidy was awake now, but yawning, her arms above her head as if she were stretching. Gently, being careful to support her head, he scooped her up into his arms and stood there gently rocking her, smiling down at her. She was gorgeous!

'She's beautiful…'

'Yes, she is.'

He stood there for a moment, just enjoying having Cassidy in his arms, then after a bit went back to his seat and settled down with the baby in his arms.

'Have you told Connor she's been born?'

'Yes.'

He looked up at her. 'And when's he coming?'

'He's not.'

Theo frowned, feeling annoyed that this idiot of a man could walk away from such beautiful souls. 'Did he say why?'

'No. He thanked me for telling him and then said he had to go. That he'd send me some money for "nappies and things".'

Theo wanted to swear. But to do so with a baby in his arms felt wrong. 'Have you told your mother?'

Sophie nodded, but didn't smile. In fact, she looked close to tears.

He got up and walked around her bed to the cot. He laid Cassidy down before grabbing a tissue box from the side of the bed and passing it to her. 'Is she not coming either?'

Sophie shook her head, dabbing at her eyes. 'Said she was busy. That she might make it down for Christmas.'

'Then who's going to look after you?'

'I'll manage. I'll find a way. I'll—'

'I'll help.'

The words were out without him even having to think about them. For her to be so let down by Connor and her mother was appalling! And who else could she ask? She had friends, but they were all paramedics, too, and they wouldn't be able to take time off work. Theo figured he could take a couple of weeks—he could make the time up later—and after that... Well, he could bring in reinforcements. There was no way he was going to let her do this alone! It was what friends did. They were there for each other.

'No, Theo. I couldn't ask you to jeopardise your studies.'

'No jeopardy. I can make up the time. As long as I fulfil the required number of hours on placement, it doesn't matter when I get them done. I can help you out for a week or two. And my sisters will help—I know they will. Don't you worry about anything. I'll sleep on the couch,' he added, to clarify.

Not that he needed to. They were just friends. She wouldn't expect anything else of him— he'd made his position clear.

'Theo…you're so…so good to me. Thank you.'

He smiled at her, feeling good about his sudden decision, even though his logical brain was screaming internally at him—*You're doing what?*

CHAPTER TEN

SHE'D NEVER IMAGINED returning home like this—on crutches, hobbling up her front path whilst, behind her, her student carried Cassidy in her car seat. It wasn't meant to be like this. She'd never imagined coming home truly alone, having figured Connor might show up out of guilt, at least! Or her mother… But the less said about her, the better.

Of all the people she could rely on, it was Theo.

Handsome, caring, lifesaving Theo.

A man she couldn't have.

A man you don't want. Remember?

Though right now she was struggling to remember why. Something to do with commitment and responsibilities? But if that was the case then what was he doing here? Was he just being reliable and dependable, as he'd promised?

Of course he is. It couldn't possibly be anything else.

Theo didn't want this kind of responsibility full time! He was doing this out of pity, or something. Kindness, maybe.

'It's good to be home,' she said.

'I bet.'

Theo placed Cassidy down in the middle of the floor in Sophie's living room and they both just stood there for a moment, looking down at her.

'What do we do with her now?' she asked.

Theo shrugged and said nothing, but then a bubble of laughter escaped him and, before they knew it, they were both laughing hysterically.

Sophie hobbled over to her sofa and flopped down, propping her crutches against the wall.

'Cup of tea?' Theo asked.

'Oh, yes, please. The stuff they serve you in the hospital tastes of dishwater, at best.'

'It's a ploy—to make you go home quicker.'

'Well, it worked.'

With Theo making himself at home in the kitchen, Sophie found herself staring at her daughter, fast asleep in her car seat, and wondering just what kind of life she was going to give her. Her own experiences of life had taught her that she was always second-best, or not worth staying for. How did she want her daughter to feel? How did she want her daughter to grow up? She would do anything not to let her daughter feel that way, and that had to start now. Cassidy would know that she was loved.

But one parent would have to be enough, because Sophie really didn't see her ever having two...

'Here you go.' Theo brought her a cup. 'She'll be ready for a feed soon, won't she?'

Sophie smiled. Theo knew their routine already. The time they'd spent in the hospital together had really focused him, and she'd marvelled at how dedicated he was to seeing to their needs. What would she have done without him?

But I can't rely on him for ever. He won't be here long.

'Yes, she will,' she said.

'Well, I'll go and unpack everything upstairs whilst you take care of that.'

She was breastfeeding, and she'd noticed that Theo would discreetly disappear whenever she needed to feed Cassidy. He didn't need to. She would cover herself with a shawl or blanket if she wanted to. But she said nothing. Theo was coping with this in his own way and she didn't want to start telling him what to do. He wasn't her partner. He was just helping out.

Theo got Cassidy out of her car seat and laid her in her arms.

Sophie felt her heart expand every time she looked at her. Every time she held her. Cassidy made her happy. So did Theo—but she figured that was just postnatal hormones trying to make her feel she was in a happy family, even though she knew it wasn't real.

As Cassidy latched on Sophie found herself unexpectedly wiping away a tear. The midwives had said she might feel emotional for a little while. Her body had been through a lot. It had been very traumatic. She'd been trapped, frightened, at her most vulnerable.

The fact that she was doing so well was all down to Theo.

Where would I be without him?

The doorbell rang, startling them both out of sleep. It seemed both he and Sophie had nodded off on the sofa—Theo looked at his watch—for about an hour.

'Dinner's here.'

Sophie struggled into an upright position. 'You ordered takeaway? I'm not sure I want spicy food whilst I'm breastfeeding—'

'Not takeaway.' He smiled. 'My sisters, re-member?'

He almost laughed at her confused frown, then hurried to the front door and opened it wide.

'Theo!'

Hazel, Leonora and Martha all stood on the doorstep, armed with trays and dishes of food that should last him and Sophie a good week. His heart swelled at seeing them, and he gave them each a hug before inviting them in and leading the way into the lounge.

'Soph? Meet my sisters—this is Martha, that's Hazel, and Leonora on the end.'

Sophie beamed a smile. 'Hello.'

'They've brought food, so that we don't have to think about shopping for the first week. Plus...' he smiled '...it's also an excuse for them to come and spy on the woman who's wickedly blackmailed me into staying and looking after her child.'

'Theo! That's not true!' said Martha, blushing, giving his arm a gentle, playful shove. 'Well, maybe a little true—but come on! It's not every day our dear, determinedly single brother shacks up with a woman and a baby, is it? You'll have to excuse us, Sophie, we're a little protective. Of course we wanted to help out, but admittedly we were curious, too.'

Sophie laughed. 'I get it. Don't worry—I'd probably do the same thing, too, if I had a sibling.'

Leonora passed her tray to Theo. 'Well, don't just stand there, brother mine. Put the kettle on whilst we chat to Sophie and coo over the baby.'

Theo looked to Sophie, to make sure she was okay being surrounded by his protective family, and she gave him a small wink and smiled, so he headed into the kitchen.

It was good to see his sisters again. He'd not really seen them since his placement with Sophie on rapid response. They'd spoken on the phone, obviously, but it wasn't the same as spending time with them. He'd almost forgotten how they could be when they were all together. He jokingly referred to them as 'The Coven' when they were away from their husbands and children and the wine began to flow, but it was affectionate. He loved them to pieces and hoped Sophie would like them too.

He'd asked if they wouldn't mind helping out with a dish or two, but he'd certainly not expected them to all descend at once! Not that he minded...

From the living room he heard cascades of laughter from all four women, and he thought he detected his name being mentioned. When he took the cups of tea through Martha was regaling Sophie with a childhood tale of Theo getting nettle stings all over his backside, because he'd been running around naked in their back garden and had fallen into a wild patch.

He felt his cheeks colour, but he laughed with them, because Sophie seemed to be enjoying every minute of his sisters telling her things about him she didn't know—from the time he threw up after eating all their Halloween sweets one year, to the time he held Martha's hand whilst she gave birth, because her husband hadn't been able to make it through the traffic. They also told her about how Theo had sat with Hazel and her partner David as they'd watched over their son in hospital when he'd got suspected meningitis. His dedication. His strength. His commitment to them.

He sat there mostly saying nothing, blushing sometimes, his gaze meeting Sophie's, watching her smile, watching her laugh. She fitted in with them so well, and she regaled them with some tales of her own of their time together in the rapid response vehicle.

He hadn't realised just how proud she was of him.

He felt happy. Content.

And that frightened him—because he knew happiness and contentment always got taken away from him. He'd always thought his dad was the centre of his world, until he'd learned that he was leaving. He'd thought he could look after his mum and keep her safe, until she'd succumbed to her condition and died. He'd thought he'd be able to look after his three sisters and keep them safe for ever, until they'd each flown the nest and left him behind.

Even the army—the one place where he'd thought he'd have a family—had disappeared the day he'd lost Matty-Boy and it had begun to hit home that he always lost those he allowed himself to get close to. Letting his guard down, always ended with him getting hurt.

Even this—what he was experiencing now— was a mirage. It wasn't really his. Sophie wasn't his. Cassidy wasn't his. He was only here as a stopgap, helping her out—it wasn't *real*.

The thought cast a pall which he tried to ignore.

He smiled when he felt he ought to.

He kissed and hugged his sisters goodbye and closed the door after waving them off.

When he got back inside the living room, to see Sophie about to feed Cassidy once again, he made his excuses and said he was going to grab a quick shower.

He could see that Sophie was worried about him.

Had she noticed a change in him?

Well, she didn't need to worry.

He wasn't hers to worry about.

Which was something they both needed to keep in mind.

CHAPTER ELEVEN

SOPHIE HAD *LOVED* Theo's sisters. To see the bond between the siblings had made her yearn for the same thing, wish that she'd not been an only child. But then, if she'd had a brother or a sister it would have been one more child to be ignored by their mother, so it was best that it had been just her.

Though it might have been a little less lonely…

She envied the relationship Theo had with Martha and Leonora and Hazel. They were so close! And she'd loved having them here. Such a noisy, but loving group…

Would Cassidy ever have a sibling? It might be nice for her to have one, if they could be anything like Theo and his sisters were together, but that would entail trusting a man enough to be in her life and she wasn't sure she could do that.

Theo was the closest she'd come to letting a

man back into her life again, and she could see he would make a great father—

No! Stop it!

Maybe this was a bad idea, having Theo so close all the time? So available? So giving of himself? It didn't tally with all that he'd told her of not wanting commitment, and yet here he was! Unless he thought of her as family? A kind of sister, perhaps?

Now, why does that thought depress me?

'Because I don't want him to see me as a sister, do I, Cassidy?' she said quietly, picking up her daughter. 'I want him to see me as a woman.'

Cassidy opened her mouth, rooting for a feed.

'I don't know why. It's just how I feel and… and I think that's okay. Because he saw me as his boss and his mentor, and then he saw me give birth, for crying out loud. You can't get any more intimate than that, huh?'

He saw me give birth.

She'd read somewhere online that some men didn't want to watch their wives give birth in case it put them off having sex with them. Which seemed a ridiculous, misogynistic thing for any man to say.

She wondered if men really were so fragile that they needed to maintain the fantasy that their wives and girlfriends' vaginas were only for their sexual pleasure—not a place that could get torn or ripped as a baby squeezed itself out. She almost laughed. It was ridiculous, whatever it was.

Theo had watched her give birth and he hadn't looked appalled or embarrassed. He had been concentrating on the task at hand, had tried to maintain her dignity, and he had marvelled at the new life she had brought into the world.

Besides, he's not sexually attracted to me. We almost kissed that time, but he stopped it. Saved me from embarrassing myself. And, quite frankly, I'm embarrassing myself still now, if I even think that for one moment he's thinking of me in such a way!

Theo couldn't stop thinking about Sophie. She was in his head constantly.

Was she feeling okay?

Had she taken her painkillers?

Was her leg comfortable?

Did she need anything to eat?

Did she need help getting upstairs?

What did she think of his family?

Had she enjoyed the visit with his sisters?

Why did he feel that they had something special between them when she winked at him?

Why did he enjoy her smiles?

Why did her happiness and contentment make *him* feel so good?

His mind was whirling with all the possibilities and he couldn't quite get a fix on his emotions.

When he'd said he'd help out he'd meant it, figuring that sleeping on her sofa for a few weeks wouldn't be a problem. He could help out with laundry, do the shopping, run errands, hold the baby on occasion when Sophie needed a break... But he found himself doing a whole lot more. Looking at Sophie in snatched moments. Thinking about her. Wondering if he could reach out and just take her hand... What it would have been like if he'd kissed her that time...

He'd not been able to get to sleep at all tonight, tossing and turning on the sofa, and now he could hear Cassidy crying.

Cassidy slept in a cot attached to the side of Sophie's bed, so he knew that Sophie would be able to reach her and see to her needs in the night. Each evening he made sure that the changing bag was full, so if Cassidy needed a nappy-change Sophie could do that, too, without having to get out of bed.

But Cassidy wasn't stopping crying.

He could hear Sophie, trying to soothe her,

but for some reason Cassidy continued to cry, wailing and screaming as if nothing was going to settle her.

As soon as he heard Sophie getting upset, too, he threw off the blanket and pulled on some jogging bottoms and raced upstairs. He paused outside Sophie's room, about to knock gently on the door.

Would she be offended if he suggested that he help? Would she think he was implying she couldn't cope on her own? He'd hoped that by setting up her room each night he was empowering her to be the mother she wanted to be, that it was only her leg in a cast that was stopping her.

But Cassidy sounded miserable—and Sophie did too.

'Cassidy, please stop crying. I don't know what you want!'

Theo knocked and popped his head inside. 'Are you decent?'

He held his hand over his eyes in case she was in a state of undress, or trying to feed Cassidy without a blanket covering her modesty. Not that he'd be bothered by seeing her breast-feed. It was the most natural thing in the world. But he was aware of his intense sexual attraction to Sophie, so that made him respect her.

'I'm fine. But she won't stop crying, Theo!' And she burst into tears, too.

Theo rushed over. 'Does she want a feed?'

Sophie shook her head.

'A nappy-change?'

'I just changed her.'

Sophie grabbed a tissue from the box at the side of her bed and noisily blew into it.

'Want me to try and settle her?' he asked.

Sophie nodded, and Theo stooped to take baby Cassidy from her arms.

Poor Cassidy had a bright red face, wet with real tears, and her little body felt tense and rigid with her frustration.

Theo stood upright and placed her against his shoulder and gently began to rock her, singing a song that he remembered his dad singing to him. A song that he'd heard his sisters sing to their babies when they wouldn't settle.

Two little men in a flying saucer...'

He bobbed up and down as he rocked gently from side to side, and it took a moment, but eventually Cassidy began to settle, her crying lessening to become sniffles, then nothing, as she enjoyed the rocking, bobbing motion of his body and began to relax against him.

'I don't believe it...' Sophie whispered.

'It's a magic song. Don't tell anybody—it's a secret.'

'Where did you learn how to do that?'

'My sisters. My nieces and nephews.'

At that moment Cassidy let out a deep belch, and Theo's eyes widened as Sophie chuckled in her bed, her eyes glistening with happy tears now, not sad ones.

'You're very good with babies,' she said.

'I've had a lot of practice.'

'Thank God you're here.' She smiled. 'I'm never going to let you leave.'

He smiled, but the thought scared him a little. This was only meant to be temporary, right? But a real part of him was considering the possibility of being here and looking after little Cassidy for a long, long time. And with that came the thought of what might happen between him and Sophie.

And if he allowed it to happen…if he got comfy, if he let his guard down…would it all be taken from him?

Sophie was out of bounds and Cassidy already had a father. This wasn't his child and Sophie wasn't his girlfriend! Babies played games with your mind. They made you reconsider things…they made you wonder *what if?* They made you want. They made you question your life choices.

What if Sophie and I were an item?

He wouldn't let his mind go there.

He couldn't.

Sophie stood in front of the fridge, trying to decide what to choose for her and Theo for lunch. After his help with Cassidy the night before they were both tired, and she wanted to thank him by getting him something to eat for a change. Normally Theo cooked for them.

Looking inside the fridge, she could see she had a choice of Martha's macaroni cheese or Hazel's vegetarian lasagne. She opted for the lasagne and, whilst it was heating in the oven, began to prepare a salad.

It was a bit of a nightmare, constantly hobbling from the chopping board to the sink, to rinse vegetables in the colander, but eventually, with a drizzle of balsamic and a garlic tahini sauce, the salad looked great. She even sprinkled some sesame seeds on top for presentation.

Then she stopped to consider how she might carry two plates of food and a salad into the living room.

I'll set it up on the kitchen table and we'll eat in here.

She made them a cup of tea each, and placed a jug of water on the table, too, then went to fetch Theo. But when she hobbled into the living room she noticed that Theo was reclining on the sofa, fast asleep, with Cassidy resting on his chest, fast asleep, too!

Bless... They look so sweet together. Like father and daughter.

Only he wasn't Cassidy's father, was he? Connor was. The slimeball who had dumped her when she'd discovered she was pregnant and hadn't even bothered to turn up at the hospital. *That* was the man she'd chosen as a partner. The man she'd believed would bring her a happy-ever-after. Clearly her decision-making processes couldn't be trusted.

Why couldn't she have met Theo first? No, he didn't want commitment of any kind, but at least he'd been honest about it up-front and, despite that, here he was after only knowing her for a few weeks, living in her home and helping her take care of her child.

He'd stepped up. He'd committed. Whether he wanted to accept that or not.

But he was just a friend, and moments like this one would be rare.

With that thought in mind she pulled her mobile from her pocket, opened up the camera and took a picture of the snoozing pair.

It was a perfect photo. Theo's arms were wrapped protectively around Cassidy, his head to one side, as he caught up on the sleep he'd lost last night helping her out. And helping

Cassidy. Her daughter looked totally content. As if the two of them were meant to be.

Only I can't have him. We can't have him.

'Theo…?' she said, her voice just above a whisper. She didn't want to make him jump. 'Theo?'

Slowly his eyelids opened and he squinted, looking for the source of the voice and smiling when he saw her.

He glanced down at her daughter on his chest. 'Sorry. I shouldn't have fallen asleep like that. What time is it? Want me to prepare lunch?'

Sophie smiled. 'No need. I've done it. I've come to tell you it's ready.'

'Should I disturb Sleeping Beauty here?'

He rubbed Cassidy's back and she snuffled and snuggled further into him as he scooped her against his shoulder and carried her over to the bassinet, slowly laying her down and tucking her in. She went right back to sleep.

'Mission accomplished.'

'Lunch is in the kitchen.'

'I'll be right there. Let me wash my hands.'

She hobbled her way back to the kitchen on her crutches and laid them against the wall as she sat at the table. Moments later, Theo joined her.

'Must have been more tired than I realised,' he said.

'That's okay. You obviously needed it.'

'Why don't you take a nap this afternoon?' he suggested. 'I'll take Cassidy out for a walk in her pram...get some fresh air.'

'Thanks.'

Why was he so kind and considerate? Why was he exactly as she'd imagined her partner might be as she raised a child? Taking it in turns with her, giving her time to sleep, to rest, sharing the responsibilities equally and without blame? *Why?*

'Except the health visitor is coming this afternoon at four,' she added. 'So you'll need to be back by then so she can see Cass.'

He nodded. 'Okay. This looks great, by the way.'

'It does. I must phone your sisters later and thank them again.'

'Haven't you already done that?'

'I know... But I like talking to them. It's like having sisters of my own. Mind if I adopt them?' She laughed.

'Be my guest. They'd love that.'

The lasagne was indeed delicious, and they both had second helpings. Theo made her stay seated whilst he cleared everything away, and she watched him intently, wondering why a man who was as adamant as he was against commitment seemed to be so good at it.

'You're a good man, Theo.'

He smiled as he loaded plates into the dishwasher. 'Thanks. I try.'

'No, I mean it. I could get used to this… I have to keep telling myself it's temporary. That I'm only *borrowing* you. I know I'll be okay afterwards. You know…on my own… But it'll be odd not having you around.'

He dried his hands on a tea towel and looked at her, saying nothing. 'Well, until you're back on both feet I'll be here, so you won't be losing me just yet.'

But she would lose him one day. There was no doubt about it. And she could feel the day approaching. Getting closer and closer.

It was like being stalked by something terrible. Another man she had begun to love would leave her.

It was uncomfortable to know that it wasn't just because she needed him—she was a strong, independent woman and always had been. It was the knowledge that she *wanted* him to stay.

But she couldn't bring herself to say it out loud, Because if she did that would make her vulnerable, and she didn't want to see the pity in his face as he tried to let her down gently.

She didn't want to be like her mother—chasing happiness and love in other people. Her happiness had to come from within herself, no one else, and yet here she was pining over a man.

Just as she'd told herself she would never do.

CHAPTER TWELVE

THEO WAS OUT, walking Cassidy in her pram, and his mind was going over and over what had been said after lunch.

Of course he'd love to stay! These last few days with Cass and Soph had been some of the best days of his life! They'd laughed, they'd cried, they'd watched over Cassidy, parented her like a real couple.

Babies were intoxicating—especially babies like Cassidy, with her cute smile and her wispy curls that were just the softest thing Theo had ever touched.

But he was terrified of what was happening. This yearning to stick around was becoming impossible to deal with, and everything was still so uncertain. Soph had heard nothing more from Connor—but what if he turned up suddenly and Sophie fell back into his arms? Theo would be ejected...he'd lose them both. Of course he'd step aside to give Connor a chance to bond with his daughter. She was Connor's, not Theo's! He had to remember that.

Sophie wasn't the one borrowing *him*—he was the one borrowing *them*, playing at being a happy family again, reclaiming the past he'd had with his sisters before they'd married and had children, putting off in his head what would have to happen in the future, when it got snatched away again.

They could be taken from me at any moment.

Connor could knock on that door and that would be it.

Over. Done. *Adios muchachos!*

He knew how that would feel and it scared him to death. Already he was in too deep with Sophie and her daughter, and he knew he had to back away soon. This was all too familiar—this caring for other people, knowing he would lose them, that they had never been his in the first place. His dad hadn't belonged to him, his mother had been lost much too soon, and each of his sisters had flown the nest.

He remembered that feeling he'd felt deep in his heart when he'd stood in the house all alone.

I never want to feel that way again.

But how to step away without upsetting Sophie?

How to leave without destroying the friendship and the relationship they had created?

Perhaps if he took baby steps towards giving her independence? She was getting around much better on her crutches now, she was doing well, and if he got his sisters to check in on her that would give him time to get back to his studies. To complete his placement hours.

He couldn't forget that he had a career that had been put on hold whilst he was playing at being a family man!

This wasn't his life.

It was never meant to be.

Tormented, he got back to Sophie's house with Cassidy just as the health visitor arrived, and he invited her in, calling for Sophie.

'I'm in the kitchen!'

He smiled, parking Cassidy in her pram in the hall. She was still asleep. 'You get some rest?' he asked.

'An hour.'

'Health visitor's here.'

Sophie hobbled into view. 'Oh, hi! I'm Sophie.'

'Nice to meet you. I'm Michelle.'

'Shall we go through?' Theo suggested.

With the two ladies settled, Theo offered to make a cup of tea.

'Oh, nothing for me, thanks,' said Michelle. 'I had tea at my last lady's house.'

Sophie shook her head. 'I'm fine, too.'

Theo settled down on the couch next to Sophie.

'Well, it's nice to meet both of you… How have you been, Sophie?' Michelle asked.

'Not too bad. The leg can be a bit of a hindrance, but apart from that I'm coping well.'

'Good—that's good. And how have you been feeling within yourself? Mood okay?'

Theo sat listening as Sophie and Michelle talked. Sophie wasn't alone with Cassidy. She had her midwifery team at the end of the phone, she'd got a health visitor she could call on at any time, and there were his sisters! Hazel and Sophie in particular got on really well. And of course, somewhere there was Connor. Maybe Connor's family. And Sophie's mum. Plus, she had her friends in the ambulance service. It wasn't as if he was going to leave her in the lurch.

But he knew he had to leave her sooner, rather than later—before he got ousted by someone else. Taking control of his leaving was preferable to suddenly losing them, and it wasn't as if he couldn't keep in touch! Though for a little while he might have a bit of a break…because seeing Sophie and knowing he couldn't have her was going to be a little problematic…

'And you're Dad?'

Theo tuned back in. 'What? Me? Oh, no!' He laughed. 'No, not at all… Just a friend, helping out. I'll be gone soon. Sophie's coping really well.'

He somehow needed to say it out loud. Let her know his intentions. Announce where he was, what he needed to do.

Make it clear so it's no surprise.

He didn't look at Sophie.

So he didn't see the look on her face.

He was going to leave soon.

The words slammed into her chest like a wrecking ball and she had to swallow hard and look away, pretending to straighten some magazines on a side table so that Michelle or Theo wouldn't see how affected she was by those words.

But she couldn't have been that good at hiding her feeling, because Michelle said, 'Theo, would you mind if I have a word with Sophie in private? Just to ask a few personal questions?'

'No problem. I'll check on Cassidy…take her upstairs.'

Sophie watched him go. He sounded so cheerful.

Because he'd made up his mind to go?

Did he not realise how much she needed him? Not just because of Cassidy, but because…

She loved him.

Sophie turned to look at Michelle with tears in her eyes.

'Are you okay?' asked the health visitor.

She sniffed. 'Yes. No. It's just… I knew he was only here to help me out temporarily, but he's been so good… I don't know what I'm going to do without him.'

'You should tell him how you feel.'

'I can't. I know it's not what he wants. *We're* not what he wants. Not really. I'd hate to put him in a position where he feels trapped into staying. And besides…' she laughed '… I'm full of hormones. I don't know how I really feel.' She sniffed. 'Theo has done *everything* for me. It would be so easy to think he's the answer to it all. Did you know he delivered Cassidy?'

Michelle nodded. 'I read the notes.'

'Theo isn't the type to settle down.' She smiled through her pain. Wiped her eyes. 'He doesn't want the responsibility of a family. What if I put myself out there and ask him to stay and he leaves anyway? I can't be abandoned again, Michelle. I can't!'

'Well, only you and he know how you really feel. Maybe you should start talking about the future? See what he has to say?'

'I know what he'll say. He just said it to you.

He's going to leave soon. And I'm not chasing him.'

Sophie chatted with Michelle for a bit longer, but then the health visitor had to leave. Sophie walked her to the door and said goodbye, knowing she'd have to talk to Theo, who was still upstairs.

But the fear of having him walk away from her, of having him abandon her, was just too painful to bear. She loved him. She knew she did. But he didn't want this. He'd laughed just now when it had been suggested he was Cassidy's dad and he'd mentioned leaving soon.

Perhaps it would just be best if she offered him an easy way out?

'Theo? Can I talk to you?'

She didn't want this conversation. Not ever. But she knew they had to have it. Had to have it now, before she went insane with all the *what-ifs*. Theo was already thinking of leaving—he'd said it himself—but what if he felt he couldn't raise the issue without upsetting her?

Well, she'd make it easier for him.

He appeared at the top of the stairs. 'Has she gone?'

'Yes. Look, we need to talk.'

He sighed. Nodded. 'Yes. We do, don't we?'

She watched him trot down the stairs. Waited for him to get to the bottom.

'I've asked so much of you, Theo. And you've given me everything I've ever asked for in helping me look after Cassidy. But you have your own life. And it's unfair of me to keep you from living it. You've put your career on hold for me. So I just want you to know that I'm ready.'

She needed to know what her future would be. Needed to plan. And she couldn't do that with Theo here, making everything so uncertain. If she planned this—if she took control—then she wouldn't be left behind. Not if she did the pushing away. It was for the best. For both of them. He was probably only staying here out of guilt, and that wasn't fair on him, either.

'Ready for what?' he asked.

'To do this on my own.' She took a deep breath, squared her shoulders. 'Thank you for everything. I've learned so much from you. So much about myself. My mother. The past. And I won't be like her—chasing happiness from people who aren't ready to give it. I've always looked after myself and I'm going to be fine on my own. *We'll* be fine. Honestly. You can leave us now.'

CHAPTER THIRTEEN

AT FIRST HE wasn't sure that he'd heard her right. But the look in her eyes told him everything he needed to know. Steely. Sure.

Had she needed him to go a long time ago and he'd been holding on like a needy child, desperate not to be left on his own again?

That was silly.

The very things he feared were the things he kept telling people he wanted—independence, no commitment, no responsibilities, to be a free agent.

And here they were, being offered on a plate.

He'd be able to walk away with no repercussions. Go back to uni, catch up with his placement hours at the weekend, make sure he met his targets and passed his year. Go back to being Theo, the man he'd thought he wanted to be.

Only now it was being offered to him he wasn't sure he wanted it at all.

And yet I did want it! Just this afternoon, I was thinking of how I could get my independence back!

But it wasn't what he truly wanted.

What he wanted was Sophie. And Cassidy.

He wanted a family and a home.

And, though it was terrifying to admit it, he knew that if he didn't speak the truth right now he would regret it for ever. He would lose them. Just like he'd lost everybody else. But there was a chance here to have something he wanted, and he ought to fight for it.

If she said no, then he'd walk away. But she'd asked him once before: *'If you met the love of your life would you want to settle down?'*

Back then, he'd not known how to answer, but right now he knew the answer.

He was damned sure of it.

'I don't want to leave.'

What? What did he mean?

'Theo, honestly… I'm fine, I don't need you to—'

'I don't want to go.'

This was confusing. Wasn't she giving him what he wanted?

'I don't understand…'

'Neither do I. But I've been thinking about this. Thinking about it a lot. I need you to know how I really feel, and I'd like you to listen. If you still want me to go afterwards, then I will, but I need you to listen first. Will you do that?'

She was shaking. Trembling. She had to adjust her weight on her crutches as her heart pounded madly in her chest, hoping he wasn't about to make this even more painful than it already was.

'I know what I've always said about relationships. That I don't want to settle down…that I don't see myself as being in a committed relationship. But I think that's because I've never truly been in one before where love like this has existed.'

'Love like this?' she whispered, almost afraid of the answer, but also desperately needing to hear more.

'The kind of love I have for you. And for Cassidy. I know she's not mine. And I know I can never be her real father. But I would very much like to be your real boyfriend. Your real love. The man who gets to love you every day, through thick and thin. The man who gets to see you first thing in the morning and last thing at night. The man who gets to hold you in his arms and never let go. I know you might not want me like that. I know you may think that I'm not reliable. But I am. I can't imagine walking out of that door, knowing that I can't be with you, knowing that you can only be my friend. But if that's what you need me to be—a friend—then I'll take that if that's all I can have. Being here with you and Cassidy has made me feel complete. It's made me feel whole. I want to build a future for the three of us, no matter what happens, no matter what complications or difficulties there may be ahead—because being by your side makes me the strongest and luckiest man in the whole world.'

Tears were streaming down her face. Happy tears. And her heart felt so swollen with joy in her chest that she thought it might burst right open and shower the world with rainbows and sparkles.

'You love me?'

He nodded. 'I do.'

'Oh, my God, Theo…'

She looked down at the floor, trying to gather her thoughts, trying to gather herself, to process the enormity of his statement.

This is everything I've ever wanted!

'I was trying to tell myself that I had to be happy for you to leave. I kept telling myself you were on loan and that what we had wasn't real, that we were living in a world of make-believe. I tried so hard not to fall for you, Theo, but you made it difficult! Being so sweet with me, with my daughter… I couldn't have asked for more. But I love you, and I found myself wanting more. I did. I wanted you. Wanted you to stay. And I thought by offering you a way out I'd be protecting my heart from the pain of losing you.'

He stepped closer, stroked her cheek, looked deep into her eyes. 'You don't ever have to lose me.'

She smiled, laid her hand upon his, looked up into his face. 'So, tell me again that you're staying.'

He smiled. 'I'm staying.'

'For ever and ever?' Now she caressed his face, staring longingly at his lips.

'For eternity'

'Then kiss me and don't ever stop.'

Theo smiled and slowly, tenderly, pressed his lips to hers.

EPILOGUE

'DA-DA-DA-DA-DAH!' CASSIDY BEAMED a smile at Theo as he walked in through the front door and chuckled at his surprised expression.

'She's been saying that all day.' Sophie pressed a kiss to Cassidy's cheek. 'She's been saying it all morning—like I'm nobody and I haven't been pandering to her every whim for the past eight hours.'

He put down his backpack, which looked as if it contained all the books from the university library, gave Magellan the cat a quick stroke as he pressed up against Theo's legs, and scooped Cassidy from Sophie's arms.

'Yes, sweetheart, you're saying Daddy. *I'm* your daddy. Who's a clever girl then, eh?'

Sophie watched as he inhaled her perfect scent and nuzzled his nose into the wisps of dark hair that were beginning to curl. Then he held out an arm for Sophie and hugged her tight, too.

'How's your day been?'

'Fine. I had my last appointment with the orthopaedic surgeon today and he's happy with my leg. I don't need to go back and see him any more. And he said I can start thinking of going back to work on a phased return.'

'That's great!'

'It's certainly a relief.'

They walked into the kitchen, where Theo put Cassidy down on her playmat and handed her one of her building blocks. 'Something smells good,' he said.

'African stew with new potatoes and baby vegetables.'

He went up behind her and wrapped his arms around her waist, planting a kiss on the back of her neck. 'What made you think I was talking about the food?'

Sophie laughed and turned to kiss him. 'Oops, my mistake!'

She felt so happy. Life was wonderful and she couldn't imagine anything better. She and Theo and Cassidy were the perfect little family.

Even Connor was behaving—doing his part and occasionally seeing his daughter at weekends. It had been a shock to finally hear from him, though it had quickly turned out that it had been because Connor's mother was badgering him to do the right thing, so that she could see her granddaughter on occasion.

'When does your mum get here?' Theo asked.

Sophie's mum was coming to meet her granddaughter. They'd seen each other in video calls online, but never face to face. Sophie was looking forward to seeing her mother's eyes light up at seeing and holding her granddaughter for the first time.

'I'm picking her up from the station at nine.' She glanced at the wall clock. It was nearly seven.

Theo smiled. 'Two hours. I can think of something we can do in two hours. We could do it twice. Maybe three times!'

Sophie laughed. 'But dinner's ready! It'll be ruined.'

'It'll keep—and besides, there's something I want to do first.'

He smiled and reached into his pocket, pulling out a small velvet box. He opened it to reveal a beautiful solitaire diamond ring, sparkling and catching the light.

'You have my made my life so complete. I could never have imagined that I would be so happy, and I don't want anything to ruin what we have. I love you and Cassidy so much and I want to show that to the world. Sophie Westbrook—would you do me the honour of becoming my wife?'

He sank to one knee.

Sophie gasped, clamping her hand over her mouth as tears beckoned. Happy tears. Disbelieving tears. Joyful tears. Of course she would marry him!

'Oh, my God, yes! Yes, I will!'

He smiled and slid the ring onto her finger, standing to press his lips to hers and embrace her within his arms.

She was his.

She and Cassidy both were.

The love they shared was beyond anything she had ever experienced before.

And now it was for ever.

* * * * *